QUEEN OF LIKES

QUEEN
OF
LIKES

HILLARY HOMZIE

ALADDIN M!X
New York London Toronto Sydney New Delhi

This book is a work of fiction. Any references to historical events, real people, or real
places are used fictitiously. Other names, characters, places, and events are products of
the author's imagination, and any resemblance to actual events or places or persons,
living or dead, is entirely coincidental.

ALADDIN M!X
Simon & Schuster Children's Publishing Division
1230 Avenue of the Americas, New York, New York 10020
Originally published by Aladdin, An imprint of
Simon & Schuster Children's Publishing Division.
First Aladdin M!X edition April 2016
Text copyright © 2016 by Hillary Homzie
Cover illustration copyright © 2016 by Solene Debies
All rights reserved, including the right of reproduction in whole or in part in any form.
ALADDIN is a trademark of Simon & Schuster, Inc., and related logo
is a registered trademark of Simon & Schuster, Inc.
ALADDIN M!X and related logo are registered trademarks of Simon & Schuster, Inc.
For information about special discounts for bulk purchases, please contact
Simon & Schuster Special Sales at 1-866-506-1949 or business@simonandschuster.com.
The Simon & Schuster Speakers Bureau can bring authors to your live event.
For more information or to book an event contact the Simon & Schuster Speakers
Bureau at 1-866-248-3049 or visit our website at www.simonspeakers.com.
Cover designed by Jessica Handelman
Interior designed by Mike Rosamilia
The text of this book was set in Bembo Std.
Manufactured in Canada 0316 OFF
2 4 6 8 10 9 7 5 3 1
Library of Congress Control Number 2015933126
ISBN 978-1-4814-4521-4 (pbk)
ISBN 978-1-4814-4522-1 (eBook)

TO NETTIE RUMSKY,
MY MAGICAL MARY POPPINS. I MISS YOU.

QUEEN OF LIKES

1

I Love Likes

I stare at my phone, waiting.

One second, 3 LIKES.

Five seconds, 9 LIKES.

Ten seconds, 12 LIKES. All for a photo of the sunrise I posted on Snappypic. On my screen, the sun glows like a pale egg as it rises over the mountains.

Actually, I don't love my outdoorsy shots. They're a little boring, but it's the kind of thing my followers think is cool.

So I'm okay with the setting sun if it gets me lots of LIKES.

Right now I'm hiding in the bathroom stall at my temple. And the place is packed because it's Milton P. Daniels's bar mitzvah. The bathroom is the only spot where I can have some privacy. Over in the pews, there are probably three hundred people.

Fifteen seconds, 15 LIKES! A smile tugs all the way to my ears. I want to dance.

I glance back at the phone. It's been two minutes, and I'm up to 45 LIKES. Yes! This calls for a celebration with Floyd. (That's my phone's name.)

I peer back down at my phone. But . . . wait. I'm holding steady at forty-five. Where are all my LIKES? I refresh the page. And . . .

Nothing.

I shake my phone as if that might help.

Still nothing.

This doesn't make sense. I used the filter that everyone else on Snappypic is really into. It makes everything seem dreamy. But with only 45 LIKES, the sun is losing its brilliance and looks lonely and unloved.

Maybe I need to turn it off and on?

I turn off my phone and restart it. I text Ella Fuentes: Did you see my photo? I add a smiling emoji.

No response.

♥ 2 ♥

I know Ella's up. It's late morning. She's my best friend. Maybe she's reading or drawing, but she's definitely up.

If she wasn't doing something else, I'm sure she'd LIKE my photo. I try a couple other girls I know. Nothing. It's late Saturday morning and all my followers have to be up by now.

As of 11:07 a.m. today, I have 12,032 followers on Snappypic. My followers are pretty much all the kids at Merton Middle School and a bunch of other middle schools around Portland. But I have two middle schools in Mission Viejo. That's all the way down in Southern California. I didn't know where it was until I checked it out in Google Maps. Usually between four hundred and nine hundred followers give me a thumbs-up on anything I post. So yeah, I get more LIKES than anyone I know at school.

Sometimes I have to pinch myself that this is happening to me. Last year in sixth grade, I didn't even have an account. People pretty much ignored me. Back then, I was too awkward. Too tall. Too loud. And generally uncool.

Taking a deep breath, I swipe through Snappypic and start LIKING everything my followers have posted. This is a way to get LIKES coming back.

4 isn't3

You've got to give to get.

My thumbs rifle through close-up selfies, the self-portrait shots that are so close-up you can almost see nose hair, and photos of ugly jeggings and food shots, including one of mini chocolate cupcakes with buttercream icing.

I LIKE it all, even though most of it looks like a thousand other shots.

More LIKES roll in for my sunrise photo.

Thirteen more.

Seventeen more.

Phew, the numbers are going up. A happy, bubbly feeling percolates inside me.

Time flies by as I continue LIKING more photos.

Heels clack into the bathroom. A nearby stall door clicks shut.

My phone pings. I glance down and see that Bailey Jenners has LIKED my sunrise photo. And she has messaged me!

Bailey Jenners, Queen Bee of the seventh grade.

Bailey has written: There's something I want to ask you. It's superimportant. My heart thuds in my chest as I picture Bailey, head down, birdlike and small, typing.

I want to cry with joy. Bailey LIKES my photo and

has messaged me! I know it's silly. But now, even with all my followers, sometimes I'm still surprised that people like me. Especially in real life.

I type: What? oh-so-casually, like my heart isn't a bass drum. What could she want? Bailey, who is the center of everything in seventh grade, has never messaged me before, although she has LIKED plenty of my photos. Well, everyone at Merton Middle School pretty much has by now.

My phone pings again. That's got to be Bailey responding, letting me know what she needs to tell me.

Someone bangs open the restroom door. A familiar jasmine-y scene wafts into my stall. "Karma? Are you in here? You've been in here for thirty minutes!" That's my mother's voice. She sounds out of breath. And she sounds very, *very* annoyed. "Karma, you missed it!" she yells.

Oh no! Missed what?

I stuff my phone back into my purse and slowly step out of the stall.

"Right before the service ended, they called your name. To go up to the front." Mom folds her hands in front of her dress. The sequins glimmer under the light. Then she wildly points to the door, like maybe I've forgotten how to get out of a bathroom.

UGGGH! I did totally forget about the *thing*. All the boys and girls who are having upcoming bar and bat mitzvahs were being called to help Milton P. lead a song. I blew it big-time. A bar mitzvah is a mega celebration for Jewish kids when they turn thirteen. It's almost like a wedding. But not. It's the day you officially become an adult. You do this by learning how to read Hebrew and getting up in front of everyone at temple. You have to write a speech and do a community service project. Afterward, there's a big party. I know all about it since my big day is coming up soon.

Mom glares at me, her lips pursed, her hands on her hips. "What were you doing in the bathroom for so long?"

My stomach twists into a knot. A lot of kids went up and I didn't think they'd be calling us by name. Argh.

I step to the sink and wash my hands, trying for a normal bathroom-y activity. "Sorry. I don't feel that great." I dry my hands on a towel.

Mom lets out a long sigh. "Honey, you should have told me." She puts her palm on my forehead to check for a temperature.

The door to another stall flings open. Neda Grubner, temple president, clicks toward the sink in her high heels. She pouts her bright orange-y trout lips. "I see you're finally off your phone."

"Off the phone?" Mom looks at me with her very disappointed face. Her lips sag down, her forehead furrows.

Neda squirts an extra dollop of lotion onto her hands. Then she pats down her shellacked gray hair. "Oh, I heard the pings, all right."

How can she be such a tattletale? And how does she know about what the pings mean?!

Mom motions me toward her. "Karma, were you on your phone?"

"Just for a second," I mumble.

Mom motions me toward her. "Let me see it."

What? No! She can't. I think now I'm actually going to be sick.

"Karma. Now!" Mom's eyes look determined. Uh-oh. That look means business.

Moving as slowly as possibly, I pull my phone out of my purse.

I don't think I like what's about to happen.

My stats:

133 notifications

12,032 followers

3,456 people I'm following

99 LIKES on my posting known as "Sunrise Photo"

Mood: Very extra worried

2

Out of Air!

"Mom, it's not how it looks," I plead.

"Oh, really?" She scrolls through Snappypic. "Haven't been on your phone, huh? You've been on it constantly since"—she peers up at the time on the screen—"the moment you woke up this morning. This. Is. Not. Acceptable."

Heads turn in our direction. From the sink, Neda raises her perfectly shaped eyebrows. Then, with a satisfied smirk, she escapes the bathroom.

"But I—"

"No more excuses." Mom's voice is a screechy whisper.

She motions me toward the door. "I'm taking you home. You're grounded. Let's go tell Dad we're leaving."

Grounded? We're missing the entire lunch? Does she have to announce this to the entire congregation? To everyone in Portland?

My stomach twists as she drags me into the social hall. It's loud. The guests chat and laugh. Clumps of hungry people crowd around the food tables. Heaps of olives, wedges of cheese, crackers, and freshly baked challah sit on silver trays. From the looks of things, the main course will be sesame bagels and mounds of lox, the most delicious smoked salmon ever. But I will not taste a crumb of bagel or a morsel of lox.

Mom rushes toward Dad as if she's got a train to catch. Dad, in a blue suit, stands next to tray of pita, munching away. Normally he's in a tie-dyed Grateful Dead T-shirt.

Mom grabs his elbow so hard he spills a lump of hummus on his tie.

Dad brushes it off with a blue napkin that's stamped MILTON P. DANIELS. "Is everything okay?"

"Oh, honestly." Mom cleans the tie with the side of her hand.

"What's wrong?" asks Dad.

Mom pops a single pecan into her mouth and chews angrily. "Take a guess."

"Karma, were you on QuickiePic?" His eyebrows rise in a question.

"Snappypic," I correct. "Um, kind of. Maybe. Just a little." Across the room, my little brother, Toby, and his friends giggle as they blow on the pink foamy stuff from the punch bowl. Suddenly I wish I were seven again.

Dad puts his water down on the table. "Snappypic? Karma, really?" He groans as if someone has pinched him, hard.

"It's not that bad." A group of ninth-grade boys pass by and snort. My parents really want to embarrass me in front of everyone.

"Not that bad?" Dad wipes his mouth. "How many times have we talked about this?"

I don't think I'm supposed to answer that. The Steinbergs, an elderly retired couple, smile and come up to us. Mrs. Steinberg clasps my hand. "Karma, you must be looking forward to your big day. Your bat mitzvah's coming up soon too."

"Very much so," snaps Mom. "So sorry," she murmurs, "but we need to leave. A little family emergency."

Emergency? Me being on Snappypic is suddenly an

emergency? On the opposite wall, a fire extinguisher hangs in a glass box. Now *that's* for real emergencies. Snappypic? Most people would be happy their daughter is that well-liked.

"I'm sorry to hear you have to leave." Mrs. Steinberg pats Mom's shoulder sympathetically as if a relative is sick or something.

Dad tells Toby that he'll be right back, and soon enough, the three of us are in the entry hall, standing next to a basket full of programs. My parents glare at me as if I just robbed a bank.

Floyd pings inside Mom's purse. Another text or maybe a message on Snappypic. Maybe from Bailey. A few people chat on the other side of the entryway.

Dad gestures to the front entrance. "Let's go outside."

Mom opens the door and I go to follow them, but Dad shakes his head. "We need to talk alone. Just for a bit."

Through the glass doors, I see them conferring on the front patio. The sky is ice blue. A cool breeze makes the leaves on the bushes rustle, but there are no rain clouds in sight. Grimacing, Mom tucks her shoulder-length brown hair behind her ears. Their heads are bent down together, whispering furiously. What can they be saying? Mom turns and motions for me to come outside too.

I push open the door and join them. All at once, they sigh deeply, as if an unspeakable tragedy has just occurred.

I send out calming vibes. "What?" I ask.

My parents study me in this scary way, and I know I won't like what is coming next.

"You lied, Karma." Mom's voice rises. "Are your . . . 'fans' this important?"

"Followers. They're called followers," I correct her. "Not that it matters," I add hurriedly after seeing her face.

"This is what I know." Mom slaps her hands on her hips. "You've lost our trust."

Dad's face scrunches. "Karma, it was the middle of a bar mitzvah. You're going to be up there soon. And even if you weren't . . ." He trails off.

Mom shakes her head. "Your behavior is unacceptable. We've gone over this before. Many, many times."

Dad ticks off a list on his fingers. "You're on Snappypic when you're supposed to be asleep. You're on it at dinner. You've been caught three times in class. We've given you lots of chances."

"A thousand," says Mom. "You don't pay attention to your brother anymore. You obviously weren't paying attention today, and—"

"Was too. Ask me anything about the bar mitzvah.

I'll prove it." I glance up at Dad, hoping he'll take my side on this. But he frowns, and his frown turns into a scowl as Mom's purse pings from my phone getting another message.

I wonder if that's Bailey again. I'm dying to find out what she wants.

Mom yanks Floyd out of her purse. She holds it in her hand like it's a hot potato. "I'm shutting this thing off." My eyes pause on my screen. I can almost see who the text is from.

Almost. But Floyd is backward. My insides tighten. If I were a rubber band, I'd snap and whizz across the parking lot.

My raspberry blingy case glistens in the sunlight. Mom turns the phone off. I swallow hard. "Mom! You don't understand—"

"No, it's you who doesn't understand." Mom's mouth becomes a hard line.

"So we've come up with a new punishment," says Dad. "Something that will get your attention."

Dad looks at Mom and Mom looks at Dad, and I can tell that they are a united front against me. "We're going to close your Snappypic account," states Dad.

"What?" My stomach dips as if I've just dropped from the highest part of a roller coaster. I want to flop against the nearest car in the parking lot. "You can't do that. It's *my* account. It's private. You can't." Every day I get smiley faces and hearts and balloons and LIKES. All of the time. Waking up and not being able to see what my followers are up to? Being totally cut off like that? My parents might as well send me to Antarctica because I'm going to be frozen out of everything. "This must be some kind of hallucination," I say. "The parents I know would never do this to me!"

"Karma, I'm sorry," says Mom. "But I think you are overreacting. You knew the rules."

"Please." I clasp my hands together. "Please, please. *Please*. I'll do anything. I'll babysit Toby as much as you want. I'll clean the house every single day. I'll make dinner. I'll—"

"It's a final decision," says Dad.

"But I'm like . . . a professional. I have more followers than some companies."

"Exactly our point, Karma," says Mom. "You're not a company. You're our daughter and still a kid. And I don't really love this obsession of yours."

The parking lot is practically spinning. "You just don't want me to grow up!" I fling up my arms. "Please," I beg. "Don't do this." My eyes water. In the past, my parents have taken away Floyd for a few hours, an afternoon, and even a weekend. But closing down my account? That's just plain cruel. "I need it! I have over ten thousand followers," I plead to Dad, but he folds his arms in front of his tie and jacket.

I stare at Floyd as Mom grips him so hard her knuckles are white. "We're also taking this away."

"What?!" I reel back. "How can I live without a phone? That's not fair!"

"We had an agreement, Karma," Dad reminds me. "You got all *A*s and *B*s on your final report card last year, so you got your new iPhone. And you got Snappypic. But that also meant following rules. Like putting away your phone after nine. And no phone at the table, and . . ."

"It's not just about today," adds Mom. "It's just gotten out of control. All you do, day and night, is go on that QuickiePic."

"Snappypic!" I swallow hard.

That's when Toby pads into the parking lot, his tie totally askew.

"Toby! What you are doing here?" Mom says.

"Please go back in there." She points to the synagogue.

"I don't like being by myself," he squeaks. By himself? There are hundreds of people inside.

"We'll only be a minute," says Mom. "Go back inside and find your friends."

"Honey, go back in the there," says Dad. "I'll be there in a second."

Mom kisses Toby on his forehead beneath his mess of curls. Toby reluctantly meanders back into the temple. Even outside, I can hear people cheering, applauding. They sound so happy.

They sound deafeningly happy, and I think I'm about to cry.

"Please, *please*! I'll do anything."

Mom bites her bottom lip. And for a moment, she looks like Cool Mom, who once in a blue moon buys me not-on-sale shoes. She rubs her forehead and sighs. "For emergencies, we'll buy you one of those pay-as-you-go phones."

"A flip phone? You've got to be kidding me!" Now the tears flow. Don't my parents get how rare it is at my age, at any age, to have 12,032 followers? Do they want me to go back to being Unknown and Unliked Karma, otherwise known as Bad Karma?

Mom stalks toward our car, gripping my phone so tightly in her hands it looks like it's about to liquefy. "This is going into hiding," she calls out. "If you have good behavior, we'll consider giving it back to you sometime in the future."

"Mom, don't!" I race after her into the parking lot. "Bailey—I have to message her! Give it back!" My heart thuds in my chest. I race up to try to peel it out of her hands.

"Not happening. I'm sorry, but you need a break from this." And with that, Floyd disappears into Mom's purse.

My stats:

12,032 followers, but not for long

5,456 people I'm following, but also not for long

3 messages, probably from Bailey, that I can't respond to

2 fascist parents

1 doomed life ahead

Mood: Worst ever

3

Steamed!

I can't believe my Snappypic is gone. My parents destroyed it in a few quick swipes. There's no way I'm ever talking to my parents for the foreseeable future. It's Sunday, and I'm stuck doing dishes. I'm not sure what happened to Saturday since I spent the rest of the day after the parking lot disaster mostly in my room, in my bed, buried in my quilt. Well, I read a book. It's not like I could call anyone, since I have no phone. It's not like I could see anyone, since I'm grounded. Later this afternoon, Dad's buying me a pay-as-you-go phone. But that doesn't count.

I grab a dish out of the sink. It's coated with something crusty and yellow. Probably eggs, judging from the shell in the sink. No matter how hard the water spurts out, the yellow mess clings to the plate like an egg leech, not letting go. I'm forced to get out the sponge and rub, not with the soft side but with the rough side. With every ounce of strength, I erase the egg off the plate. I think of my Snappypic. It's gone just like the egg.

In the nearby family room, Toby's laughing. He's watching his favorite show, *Bunny Rangers*, or something like that. I rinse off the plate. I think about all my lost comments. All my photos. All my LIKES on Snappypic down the drain.

Grabbing the plate, I dry it with a checkered dish towel. My hand rubs in a circle so fast the plate heats up. It's so hot that maybe it will combust. Right now, I'm spinning. Maybe I'll combust too.

I really, really want to talk to Ella. I need my best friend. Now. My hand reaches for the phone next to the pencil canister, but it's not there. Right. Three weeks ago, in a money-saving move, Mom got rid of our landline. I can't believe it. Why didn't she choose the stupid dishwasher? I don't need a clean plate. I need Ella.

Taking some mugs out of the sink, I imagine my life tomorrow at Merton Middle School. I flip the mugs upside down and wedge them into the top rack. Tomorrow, will anyone say anything to me about my Snappypic being gone?

No. It's Sunday. They won't notice. Lots of kids don't post on Sunday. Or they're away for the weekend. But what about Bailey? I'm going to see her on Monday, and she's going to think I blew her off.

I grab a couple of bowls and try to balance them on the rack. I hate putting in the bowls. They never quite fit.

So tomorrow I can almost pretend it's a normal day. Ella will be at school. Just thinking about telling my best friend makes me feel a little less horrible. Ella always knows how to make me feel better. One time when I was feeling down, she made me open up a present. When I unwrapped it, there was a box. And then another box. And another. And then inside the smallest box there was a paper rainbow heart. And on it, in calligraphy, she had written, *Karma Cooper is the best BFF.*

I can't wait to see Ella. That's going to be the only good thing about Monday.

My stats:

0 followers

0 people I'm following

0 friends I can call

0 friends I can visit

2 parents I'm not speaking to

1 Monday ahead

Mood: Very frustrated with the injustice of my parents!

4

What Really Happened?

Sixth, seventh, and eighth graders stand over by the morning drop-off circle, milling about, laughing, and talking to each other. But most kids haven't arrived yet since the first bell won't ring for another fifteen minutes.

I wave at Ella, who stands by our meet-up spot next to the water fountain.

"Hey," she asks, walking toward me. "You didn't answer my texts this weekend. Something wrong?"

"Um, yeah. Something hashtag *huge*. Something horrendously huge." I raise my voice over the shouts of good-byes from parents in their vans and SUVs as their kids spill out.

"What?" She shrugs off a long-sleeved shirt to reveal a much tighter cropped one underneath. Her mother would die if she saw it. "Did your phone fall into the toilet?"

I shake my head and try to pat down my flyaway hair.

"You stepped on your retainer?"

"Nope."

"Toby was snooping around your room again?" Ella leans in, examining me, and her long, almost-black hair tickles my shoulder. "You look all pale. Do you feel okay?"

"Not really," I say, my voice shaking. I tell Ella everything. She listens attentively, her soft brown eyes growing bigger with each horrible detail. She gives me a long, long hug. "So it's all because of going to the bathroom?"

I start to laugh even though I feel like crying. We pull apart and a knot of kids brushes past, all of them glancing down at their phones. I hope they know how lucky they are to have them.

"I'm so sorry," says Ella. "What are you going to do?"

"I don't know." I wince thinking about Floyd smothered in some sock drawer, sending out an SOS.

"And even worse than that, no Snappypic." I take out the lame flip phone my dad got me on Sunday afternoon. "This is all I have. Flippie." I pull it open and stare at it. "No camera. No phone. No Internet."

"Harsh."

"It doesn't even get texts." A group of sixth-grade boys mills past us. They look all wide-eyed, like they still can't believe they're in middle school, even though it's already March.

"Why would your parents actually cut off your Snappypic? That's evil. All for what? It's not like you got a suspension or something."

Some kids turn their heads. A couple of band girls flick their chins over at me and whisper. I bet everyone is wondering what I've done wrong. My old nickname, Bad Karma, is about to come back any moment, I'm sure.

I can thank Auggie Elson for that. He started calling me Bad Karma after a series of unfortunate incidents. I used peanut butter to get gum out of Bailey Jenners's hair. The gum kept on sticking.

And then the peanut butter got stuck too.

And horrifyingly, so did my nickname: Bad Karma.

It didn't help that I stepped on Lia Clark's contact

lens. And last year I told my social studies teacher I knew Ukrainian when I could only say hello, and she asked me to give a tour to a visiting teacher from Kiev. Let's just say that I did a lot of sign language.

I get all steamed up just thinking about Auggie and the possible return of my horrible nickname. What if everything I've worked for will be wiped away and forgotten?

Ella looks at me in concern and quietly says, "Let's go sit by the tables."

I nod, wondering how my best friend can always read my mind. I don't know what I'd do without her. The picnic area is in the center of the courtyard, and it's the perfect place to chill before school starts. As we skirt around the crowd and head to the quad, Ella dabs her lips with watermelon lip gloss and coats her lashes with mascara—two things her mother would never approve of. She's really strict. With her skinny jeans, cool top, and now-thick lashes, Ella could pass for someone a lot older.

"Do I look all right?" she asks hesitantly as we pass by a table of PTA moms selling reusable lunch totes with our school logo.

"Are you crazy? You look awesome." I can't help but

feel proud that she's my best friend. It's weird, but Bailey and her entourage, who we call the Bees—Janel Bryant and Megan Bogdanoff—aren't nearly as pretty as Ella, but they're way more confident. Ella isn't always so sure of herself, but she should be.

As we get closer to the picnic tables in the quad, we pass by none other than Milton P. Daniels. "Hi, Milton," I say. "You did a really good job on Saturday."

"My name is Milton P.," he corrects. Not "Thanks." Not "Thanks for coming to my bar mitzvah."

Ella shrugs and I shrug back. Nobody knows what the *P* stands for. He marches rigidly forward as he holds his mysterious shoe box in front of him. Since the beginning of sixth grade he has carried it around. His glasses get dark in the sun so you can't exactly see his eyes. Which is too bad, because they are green with yellow rings. They look like planets.

Ella nudges me with her elbow. "Do you think he could be, like, an alien spy?"

"Uh-huh. He's investigating what's in our school meat loaf for some secret space guy documentary."

"I'm serious." Ella laughs and lowers her voice. "What do you think he keeps in that box?"

"Something gross, probably. Snake skin?"

"Or a real snake."

"A baby alligator." And we're both giggling, and I'm feeling normal-ish. Ella glances at her cell. "We still have a few minutes before the first bell rings."

I glance up at a banner being put over the front entrance by a maintenance guy, and I get excited.

SPIRIT WEEK COMING SOON!

A bunch of kids point up to it, chatting. A few even clap.

"Do you think seventh grade will win this year?" I ask.

"Doubtful," says Ella. "Eighth grade always wins."

Each class gets points for participating in Spirit Week events such as the canned food drive, Crazy Hair Day, and the hot dog–eating contest. The Spirit Rally is on a Friday, and that's when the Spirit Stick is presented to the winning grade. If you win the Spirit Stick, then everyone in your grade gets a free pizza and ice cream sundae party during lunch.

Stretching, I set my backpack down on the bench and sigh loudly.

"What is it?" asks Ella.

I gaze down at the crisscross patterns of the yellow metal table. "Did you text me at, like, seven o'clock this morning? My phone is buried somewhere in my parents' room. But this morning when I went in there, I heard a text come in. Which was really weird since my parents had turned my phone off."

Ella unzips a case of colored pencils. She's an artist, so she always has them with her. "I texted you. But earlier. Like six thirty. I wanted to know what you thought about this." She taps her dragonfly earrings, which look great, of course.

I shiver and glance behind me. A few kids are on their phones. Ella sketches a girl with long, flowing green hair in her notebook.

"I need to borrow your phone," I say.

She glances behind her as if there are federal agents ready to snatch her phone out of her hands. "Just don't get caught." I have been caught with a phone during class three times and in the halls twice. So far I've gotten two warnings and three detentions for it. If I get caught again, I will automatically get an in-school suspension, which is the last thing I need right now.

I go into Ella's account and check to see what's going on. We share some of the same followers. Except she only has 587 followers. And I helped her get most of them. I scroll through. Not too much new stuff. But there's a bunch of weekend photos she hasn't LIKED yet, so I do it for her.

Ella scoops out a pink pencil and sketches a mermaid with a swanlike neck and shark fins.

I lean over and admire her drawing. "Love all the details, like the sea-star barrette. Awesomeness."

She smiles. "Really? I don't know. I'd really love to be in charge of the Spirit Week posters and stuff this year. But I don't know if people would like my stuff or how to get on the committee."

"Of course people would love your stuff," I say. Not too many people know how good she is at drawing. Ella is in band, not art, because her mother makes her play the flute. She's insecure about her art for no reason, though.

When the first bell rings, we get up to go to advisory, Merton's version of homeroom. I have Mr. Chase, who is six foot six and scares me because I think he's part giant and part psychic. Most of the boys think he's crazy and therefore love him.

A trio of girls brushes past us in the hallway. "Put your phones away," one hisses. The girls whip their phones back into their pockets. "Mr. Morley is down there." Our heads turn to glance down the hall, where the feared in-school suspension teacher stands outside of his classroom. He looks like a bouncer for a club, but it's not a club anyone wants to go to. Black paper covers the inside of the glass window in his door, because it's not so much a classroom but a jail.

Another girl, Selma Landers, who's in my gym class, high-fives me. "It's Awesome Karma!" she shrieks. It's been like this all year. My popularity online has moved offscreen and jumped into real life. I'm still getting used to it.

And now, soon enough, I'm going to have to get un-used to it.

"How many followers are you up to today, missy?" asks Selma.

I bite my lip. "Haven't been keeping count." That is no lie because there is nothing to count!

Out of the corner of my eye, I notice a cute boy who struts toward us in the hall. My stomach gets that butterfly-ish twinge-y feeling. He's got an athletic build and a lopsided grin. Quickly, I try to smooth down my hair.

Twenty feet away, he gazes at me and the butterflies are escaping and going wild now.

He gets closer. I look up at him and he looks at me . . .

And wait a minute. Hold up!

That boy is Auggie Elson. Okay, he might be cute, but cute doesn't cut out the fact that he's annoyed me for years.

And then Auggie smirks and says, "Hola, Bad Karma." Like my name is a song.

A warning bell rings. And I singsong back, "Hola, Ugh-ie," because it's all I can think of, and it's what I always say to him. Suddenly I'm extra annoyed by his twinkly sky-blue eyes, the confident grin on his face, and his strut.

Auggie Elson has no reason to strut. He should slink. He shouldn't try to be seen. His orange ukulele is strapped to his back like it's a weapon and not the silliest-looking instrument on the planet because he's plastered it with stickers. And he's a Snappypic phony. He has five thousand something followers, but he also follows that many. He'll follow anyone to get followers. I, for one, am very careful to keep the ratio of people I'm following to the number that are following me very low. That way it doesn't look as if I forced people to follow me. Well, that's what I used to do, anyway. Back when I had my Snappypic.

But that's not Auggie's way.

He doesn't care that people know he wants attention. Last year he wore a rainbow-colored beanie with earflaps to school every day because he thought it made him look cool. Believe me, it made him look weird, especially on days when it was warm.

The only good thing about Auggie is that he's in eighth grade, which means he's not in any of my classes.

This morning Auggie is beanieless and walking next to his buddy Justin Crews, who's square and bulky like a football player, and his friend Graeme Lafoot.

"Bye, Karma!" Auggie moans as if I'm embarking on the *Titanic*. I march over to him and decide to step on the back of his shoe and give him a flat tire.

Only he sidesteps and I stumble back, banging against the wall.

Justin and Graeme laugh and snort.

Auggie calls out, "Are you okay?" But I know he doesn't mean it. His sky-blue eyes are laughing.

My Stats:

0 followers, at least last time I checked, which now feels like centuries ago

0 people I'm following, which is cool since it looks better to keep that number low-ish. And it's low, all right!

0 likes. At least it's not a negative number
0 texts that I know of
1 hallway crash by Auggie, who has no right to exist
1 awesome BFF who sketches sea stars and mermaids
that fly in the sea

Mood: Annoyed anytime Auggie is nearby

5

It's Time!

After first period Bailey and the Bees catch up with Ella and me by our lockers. Bailey's got her chin-length brown hair neatly tucked behind her delicate ears. She wears her signature scarf, a pair of skinny jeans with a simple white scoop-neck tee, and glittery flats. She's so tidy and small that she makes me feel large and rumpled. Immediately I'm patting down my hair and trying to shrink myself. I should explain to her why I didn't answer her back on Saturday. I should. But I don't want to.

"Look what's hot off the press," says Bailey, nodding at the stack of fliers under her arm. Like always, she enunciates every word so that they stand out. Both Megan and Janel smile knowingly. Megan holds a stack of fliers under her arm against her hoodie. Janel carries a smaller stack in a glittery folder the same color as her caramel-colored skin.

Bailey hands papers to both of us. "Read this, girls."

SPIRIT WEEK ONLY TWO WEEKS AWAY!

Merton Middle School's largest and most fun Student Council event is called SPIRIT WEEK! The Student Council is responsible for choosing a theme for the week, designing grade-level competitions, and advertising and working events. Spirit Week includes themed dress-up days, a canned food competition among the grades, a poster contest, the spirit assembly, and a school dance.

The festivities start Monday, March 19, and end on Friday, March 23.

Student Council members take tremendous pride in their school and work hard every day to make Merton Middle School a better place.

To volunteer, come to the planning meeting after school on Monday, March 5, in room 207.

Contact Student Council Advisor Mrs. Grayson with questions.

"Cool." Ella stares eagerly at the flier as if it's coated in chocolate.

"I know. I can't wait." Bailey opens her mouth and out comes her high-pitched musical laugh. "This year, for the first time *ever*, seventh grade is going to win the Spirit Stick. I'm so excited. It's all I could think about all weekend." Her hazel eyes are bright and expectant. "We're so going win. Did you guys have a good weekend?"

"Uh-huh," says Ella in her quietest, sweetest voice. She glances at me significantly. "But not everyone did."

Suddenly I want to kill my best friend. If people don't know about my Snappypic yet, I'd rather not go there. I busy myself licking my fingers and patting down my hair. But now everyone is looking at me like they know something is up.

Bailey studies me curiously. "What's going on, Karma?"

"My parents closed my Snappypic," I say as fast as

I can. "They also took my phone. And gave me this." I show them my flip phone, Flippie.

Bailey clamps her small, delicate hand to her small, delicate mouth. "No way. You of all people. Wow. On Sunday, I tried to LIKE something of yours. But I couldn't find it. I thought it was some kind of error or something. That's crazy."

"I know," I say.

"I'd die," says Megan in her sweet baby voice. "I mean it. They could just put a gravestone up right now. Because not having my phone would be like"—she pauses—"not existing at all."

"I'm so sorry," Janel says loudly over the chattering crowd in the hallway.

"That's awful." Bailey gives me a hug and so does Megan. The hugs feel good. Bailey must really like me and has forgotten about the peanut-butter-in-hair incident. "It's too bad your parents did that. Because we were going to ask you to be publicity chair of Spirit Week for the seventh grade."

What?! I can't believe this. That's probably why Bailey had been messaging me on Saturday. My stomach drops. Why would this awesome offer have to happen the *exact* time that my phone gets taken away?

And my Snappypic gets shuts down? Coincidence? Bad Karma?

At the very least, there are definitely antipopularity forces conspiring against me.

Bailey sighs. "Oh, well. We'll have to ask someone else." She neatens the rest of her stack, which I didn't think was possible since it already looked perfectly tidy. "We need someone who can get the word out with social media in all kinds of creative ways. Basically to get the seventh grade all geared up to win."

I lock eyes with Ella. "Ella could do it," I say.

My best friend looks at me gratefully. Her cheeks glow pink. Her eyes widen. A bunch of kids swirl around our little cluster in the hall. They're trying to overhear what we're saying as we head to class.

Ella clears her throat. Her eyes dart nervously around the group. "It's a big job," she says in a whispery voice, "but I could probably get the word out on Snappypic." She shrugs. "And do posters. I'm okay with drawing and hand lettering and stuff."

"More than okay," I say. "She's amazing. She can do script so it looks like a wedding invitation, and she can draw *anything*."

"Well, maybe," says Bailey.

But Bailey is still not looking at Ella, who is standing there so cutely and artistically and sweetly. Ella, who looks like a cover girl. No, Bailey—the center of everything seventh grade—is looking forlornly, regretfully, at me.

The Break

After second period, there's a ten-minute break and I go to the bathroom. I'm in the stall when I hear familiar voices enter the washroom. Voices who say "super" a lot. Bailey, Megan, and Janel, of course.

"So what do you think of Ella?" somebody says as a toilet flushes. It sounds like Janel. My ears perk up and I quiet my breathing.

"People, there's no way that Ella can chair publicity," says Bailey.

"Well, for one thing, you can't hear her speak," says Janel. "She's so quiet."

"Exactly," says Bailey, speaking in her supercrisp way.

"Hello, I'm Ella Fuentes and I speak just like"—Megan lowers her voice even more—"a mouse."

It's true that Ella has a soft voice, but it still makes me mad to hear them making fun of her like that. I want to burst out of the stall. I want to scream at them to shut up.

But my pants are kind of down, plus I don't want to make a huge scene.

"Hey, you guys, Ella's an awesome artist," says Janel. "I'm serious. We're going to be hearing from her someday. She's like Picasso."

Okay, maybe they aren't all so vile.

Bailey laughs. "I'm sorry, girls, but there's no way Ella could handle chair. Karma would have been great. It was sick how many followers she had. With her, I'm sure we could have won the Spirit Stick."

Even though my stomach is twisting, I can't help feeling a little bit happy.

"Karma's like a super Snappypic genius. We really, *really* needed her. Too bad she can't do it. Auggie Elson is in charge of publicity for the eighth grade."

I almost choke because if Auggie does something, he does it big. Annoyingly big.

"Really?" says Megan. "That's so not good." The faucet spurts out water as someone washes her hands.

"I know," says Bailey. "And he has as many followers as Karma. Or had."

"That. Is. So. Not. True!" I scream. "I had over six

thousand, three hundred and forty-three more follow-ers! Not that I'm counting."

"Karma?" asks Bailey, knocking on my stall. "Is that you?"

Whoops. Didn't really mean to say that out loud. I get myself presentable and fling open the stall door. "In person."

> UH-OH!

"So you heard . . . everything," Bailey says. Her cheeks blush a pale pink. Bailey, Megan, and Janel crowd up by the mirror and a sixth grader with pigtails stands by the faucet. Pigtail Girl darts a quick nervous glance at Bailey and rushes out the door.

"Yeah, I heard everything. I have way more follow-ers than Auggie. Well, had. Anyway, he cheats to get his.

"If I were publicity chair," I continue, "it'd be an all-out war between two people: Karma Cooper versus Auggie Elson."

"And don't forget the sixth grade," says Janel, wav-ing a lip gloss in the air.

"Rookies don't count," says Megan in her babyish voice, which makes even mean things sound nice.

"True," I say. "They're still working on memorizing their locker combinations." Everyone laughs. I raise my arm over my head and pump my fist into the air.

Suddenly an idea hits me.

I look straight at Bailey. "I think I can be publicity chair, even without my phone."

"But what about not having a real phone?" asks Megan, popping a piece of gum into her mouth.

"Or your Snappypic," says Janel.

I clear my throat. "Well, Ella has Snappypic. Just make her my cochair." I fold my arms in front of my chest.

"We've never had cochairs before," says Megan, who raises her very plucked eyebrows. She glances significantly at Bailey. "Am I right?"

Bailey presses her hands together to make a little steeple. She purses her lips. "We've never done it before."

"Don't worry. I'll really be the chair. I can use Ella's phone. And Ella can do some art."

Bailey winces as if the thought of doing something different might be painful. Suddenly her long, dark eyelashes flutter. Her eyes are shining. "I think that"—she straightens her scarf—"I think that it's a solid idea."

"Awesome," I say, my heart skipping a beat.

"I know." Bailey high-fives me. "It'll be super. Right, girls?"

"Right," echo both Megan and Janel.

Bailey stares at me intently. "So you'll both need to go to all of the meetings."

"Sure. No problem," I promise.

"We can meet during lunch and Thursday afternoons at my house after school," says Bailey.

"Cool," I say.

Bailey high-fives me. "Super!" Her musical laugh echoes in the bathroom.

"Super! Super!" Janel and Megan echo as one twirls in front of the mirror and the other high-fives me.

We walk into the hall together, and Bailey is gazing at me like I'm her personal hero, and so is Megan and so is Janel, and everyone in the seventh grade is passing by watching Bailey and the Bees staring at me like I'm the smartest person ever. Well, Snappypic smart. And you know what? I'm feeling kind of super!

My Snappypic Fame

It all started last year at the end of sixth grade, when I posted a photo of this gopher popping out of a hole in our yard right between our Douglas fir tree and the blackberry bush. Lucky, my dog, was licking the gopher's head. Since Lucky looks like a giant four-legged Wookie, the gopher was too terrified to move. If you didn't know that, it looked as if Lucky and the gopher were BFFs. I posted to Snappypic with the caption, *Everyone needs a friend*.

And I was famous!

Soon I had a ton of followers, mostly kids from my middle school, synagogue youth group, and summer camp. Of course some of those followers weren't even real since I had opened up fifteen different accounts under different names so I could LIKE my own posts.

But my real followers *loved* that gopher photo. It landed on the popular page on Snappypic. Soon *everyone* started following me. I got 492 LIKES. And I kept on posting photos with inspiring quotes. By August I had more than 10,000 followers. And when I started school a month ago, the *whole* seventh grade was noticing me and talking about how I had so many followers and asking my opinion on everything from the best photo-editing apps to what I thought of our math teacher's hair.

Me, Karma Cooper, the girl who all throughout

fourth, fifth, and most of sixth grade was officially known as Bad Karma because I was too tall and awkward to even be a teensy bit popular. But all of that has changed. Big time.

Really Super

A moment later Ella strolls down the hallway. "Hey," she says softly. She stops and stares at all of us. My arms are linked to Bailey's and Bailey's arms are linked to the rest of the Bees and we're crazily skipping down the hall to third period.

"What's going on?" asks Ella. Her eyebrows squish together. After all, it's not every day that you see me, Megan, Bailey, and Janel skip arm-in-arm down the hall like we're about to belt out "Follow the Yellow Brick Road." Like there's a spotlight shining in a bright circle around us, announcing we're all superclose friends.

"Well, for one thing, we're going to win the Spirit Stick. Aren't we, girls?" says Bailey. She nudges me with her elbow.

I'm feeling light and airy, as if I might lift off the ground. Ella will be so happy when she hears the news about getting to cochair publicity.

I am a supergenius.

I, supergenius, gaze at my best friend and realize she still looks confused. "You and I have been picked to be the publicity chairs," I squeal.

"Really?" Her eyes grow emoji-big and her skin practically sparkles.

Everyone nods. Janel gives a big thumbs-up.

Ella jumps up and down and claps her hands and then hugs me. I'm feeling like an awesome best friend right now because I have made her dreams come true.

And mine, too.

My Stats:
2 cochairs of the publicity committee
1 real chair, but I won't tell Ella
3 Bees who think I'm a goddess, even though I don't have my Snappypic
6,343 more followers than Auggie
1 seventh-grade class that will love me when we win the Spirit Stick

Mood: Superexcited!

6

You What?

As soon as Bailey and the Bees swish around the corner to their class, Ella clutches my arm. "I'm so excited that they picked us," she says.

"Me too," I say, biting my lip. She would feel awful if she knew how much they didn't want her. "It'll be fun. We can do everything together. I mean, that's what best friends are for, right?"

"Definitely," she says. We probably have three minutes until the bell rings and we have to be in social studies.

"Can I borrow your phone?" I ask. "We need to begin our Spirit Week plan."

Ella's eyes nervously dart around the hall. "Quickly." She hands me the phone.

"I'm going to start the seventh-grade Spirit account on Snappypic. Just think of me as your"—I pause for the right word—"your assistant." I navigate over to the place where you can put up new pages and get to work.

"The bell's about to ring," says Ella.

"It's okay. Half the class rushes in as the bell rings anyway."

"Hurry." Ella glances over her shoulder through the doorway into the classroom. Most of the kids are sitting down at their desks and getting textbooks out of their backpacks. Bailey gives me a significant look as my social studies teacher, Mrs. Kirkland, sits at her desk talking to two students.

"The seventh-grade page is done," I say. "Why don't you change the banner? Make it more artsy or something?"

"Sure. I can do that," says Ella.

"I know you can." I smile and we both duck into class just as the bell rings.

The Meeting After School

Mrs. Grayson stands by the door directing kids into her classroom. Even though her name is Mrs. Grayson, she is not gray. She has bright eyes and reddish brown hair, and she's almost young, probably in her late twenties. She points to seats as Ella and I stroll through the open doorway. Around twenty students have already arrived, and they stand around in clusters, talking.

"Okay, sixth graders off to the left," Mrs. Grayson says. "Seventh graders in the middle and eighth graders over here. Council members sit in front." The desks have been pushed into a *U* formation.

"Hey, Karma. Hey, Ella!" Bailey waves at us as if we've been friends forever.

Ella grins and I wave back. The Bees point to seats behind them and we sit down. Mrs. Grayson glances at the clock. It's 3:40. School's been out for ten minutes.

"We're starting in five minutes," explains Mrs. Grayson as more students arrive. "That should give everyone enough time to get here." She confers with an eighth grader with a trendy haircut as tons of popular-looking kids filter in from the hallway to attend the Spirit Week meeting.

I glance behind me. Auggie, Graeme, and Justin swagger into the classroom. There are probably close to forty kids now, and more are trickling in. They fling their backpacks onto the ground and sit at desks or stand, gabbing with friends. Some sit on the back counter.

Mrs. Grayson leans over her desk to talk with a student but glances up. "There are a couple seats toward the front," she calls. "Don't sit on the desk. Sit on the seat." A boy with a Portland Trailblazers T-shirt trips over a backpack in an aisle. "I know it's getting crowded. Put your belongings under your desks."

A group of eighth-grade girls break into laughter as Graeme smooshes onto Auggie's lap. And then Auggie starts going "Ho ho ho" like he's Santa Claus. It's hard not to laugh at him.

Mrs. Grayson grabs a coffee mug and takes a sip. "Thanks for waiting a few minutes. I wanted to make sure everyone got here." She points to the schedule on the whiteboard:

March 5–9: Meet with your grade-
   level Spirit Week team
March 12–16: Your Spirit Week team
   publicity blitz

March 19–March 23: Spirit Week!!!!
March 23: Spirit Week dance from
   6:30–8:30 p.m. Seventh grade
   sponsors!

"Spirit Week starts two weeks from today," says Mrs. Grayson. "So you all are going to be *very* busy. It's up to you to get the maximum participation." She goes on to explain how each grade gets points for the percentage of students participating in events like the hot dog–eating contest or Crazy Hair Day.

"Hey!" A girl with pigtails in the sixth-grade section beside us springs up from her chair. "Instead of Crazy Hair, can we dress up like cartoon characters?" A bunch of eighth graders laugh and shake their heads. Kids are whispering and nudging their friends. The Bees roll their eyes, and Ella and I give each other a look.

"I don't think that's in the plans. But maybe another year," says Mrs. Grayson. "For each grade level, there will be a team with various chairs overseeing Spirit Week and one leader."

Mrs. Grayson leans on the edge of her desk. "The Spirit team leaders will coordinate everything. Could my leaders please stand up as I call out your names?" She gestures to the same eighth-grade girl with the trendy haircut she had talked to earlier. "This is Lily Pommard, leader of the eighth-grade Spirit Week team."

Hopping up, Lily waves her clipboard. I notice she has some kind of spreadsheet.

As Lily sits back down, Mrs. Grayson says, "Let's hear it for Bailey Jenners, leader of the seventh-grade Spirit Week team." We all clap. Bailey gives a big smile and smoothes her scarf.

"Next we have Gina Refrio, the sixth-grade leader," announces Mrs. Grayson. The short girl with pigtails who just asked about whether we could dress up as cartoon characters bounces up and down, waving and throwing kisses as if she's on a float at a parade. Her fellow sixth graders cheer, a few jumping up. I realize that Gina is the same pigtailed girl who I had seen in the bathroom earlier in the day. She hardly looks old enough to be in middle school, let alone the boss of something.

"Each grade will have chairs with various tasks like publicity and decoration," continues Mrs. Grayson. "After this orientation, your team leaders will tell you when and where they'll meet." She points to grade-level sections in the classroom. "We're going to break into groups in a minute, so you can let your team leader know what you're interested in signing up for. The team leaders will take it from there. Any questions?" She leans back against her desk and smiles. "Okay, so what's happening in fourteen days?"

"Spirit Week," some kids mumble. Others bounce out of their seats and scream it.

"Did you hear what I said?" She pauses for a reaction. "If you're leading Spirit Week, then Merton Middle School expects a little bit of . . ."

"Spirit," finishes Bailey. "A little woo-hoo action, people!"

"Woot!" students shout.

"Let's go, Dolphins!" someone hollers. And there's more whooping and hollering.

Mrs. Grayson's eyebrows go up as she raises her arms into the air. "So who's excited about Spirit Week?"

There's a deafening chorus of "We are!" Feet stomp. Ella and I clap our hands and glance at each other as the classroom trembles with all the whoops and cheers.

Mrs. Grayson throws back her head. A big grin breaks out on her face. "Much better. I was worried. You're leading the school, so you need to be examples for the rest of Merton. So now the big question is . . . who will win the Spirit Stick this year." She pauses dramatically. "Will it be sixth, seventh, or eighth grade?"

Kids point to themselves and clap. But the sixth graders go nuts, hopping up and down, waving their arms like a bunch of chickens. They also throw M&M's into the air and catch them with their mouths.

Auggie gets out his ukulele and starts strumming and singing, "The eighth grade 'cause we are the best. Gonna pass that Spirit Stick test. La la la la!" Some eighth graders dance to the beat.

I roll my eyes at Ella. And she rolls her eyes at me.

Even Bailey turns around and says to the Bees and us, "If they think they're going to win, they're sadly mistaken. Because we have"—she pauses as her eyes rest on me, but she says—"you guys."

Ella smiles. My heart beats extra fast. Because I know that I am the secret weapon of the entire seventh grade. I peer across the room at Auggie. I feel important, like somehow the center of the universe was happening right here in Merton Middle School because of me, Karma Cooper.

Home Sweet Home

When I get home from school, I sling down my backpack so it thuds on the floor. There's a note from Mom asking me to take the chicken out of the freezer, saying that she'll be home later than usual since she's got to pick up Toby from his friend Micah's house. Dad's out for a bike ride. Except for Lucky, who's sleeping in the family room on his dog bed, I'm all alone.

Wait a minute. I am. All. Alone. This means I can search the house for Floyd! Dashing out of the room, I dig through Mom's dresser. Dad's dresser. And their closets and the hall closet. I even swipe through the bathroom toiletries.

Nothing.

I paw through the linen closet. For years, Mom used to hide our Hanukkah presents under the quilts.

Nope.

Floyd is locked away somewhere in this house, but I have no idea where. I flop down on the couch and sigh. So close and yet so far away! Suddenly I wonder if my name is some kind of curse. Like everything I've ever done wrong is getting back at me.

But no, my name isn't bad. At least I hope not.

For a moment my eyes rest on a photo of my parents before I was born. And then a few arty portraits of Mom by Dad. My parents gave me my name because Mom getting pregnant with me was such a good thing. She and Dad had been working in San Jose in California for software companies doing sales and marketing. Then one day, Mom found out about this organic farm and yoga retreat in Oregon. If you worked there, you could live for free. So my parents sold everything and moved there. A year later, they had me. They've lived in Oregon ever since, but now in the Portland suburbs.

Karma, I guess, means "what comes around goes around," so that means my phone and hopefully my Snappypic should be coming around soon.

My Stats:
1 corny song sung on a uke by Auggie, or rather Ugh-ie
1 Spirit Stick that the seventh graders need to win
2 parents who still won't give me a break
0 idea of how many are following my new seventh-grade Spirit Week Snappypic account

Mood: Frustrated—how will I make it through this Spirit Week campaign if I can't get onto Snappypic whenever I want?

7

Up and Down

I don't see Ella at our usual meeting spot this morning, so I decide to dump books into my locker. We have half-size ones, which means you either have the bottom locker, so you're crouching, or you have the top locker and you're banging your backpack onto someone's head.

I'm the bottom locker.

Some upper-locker people are cool about being upper locker people.

Some upper-locker people have manners.

But not Auggie Elson, who has the upper locker one over from mine, which is weird. Usually the eighth graders have lockers in a separate section but somehow, for some reason, not Auggie.

It's part of Merton Middle School's policy to remind us that life is not fair.

Anyhow, Auggie Elson, of all people, now stands right over me. How did he get there so fast? He might know some secret passageway in the school or maybe he's actually an elf. His pointy ears jut out like little radar devices.

So right now I'm looking up at his ears and his annoying black-and-white checked scarf dangles into my face. He's wearing a bright aqua wool beanie. The orange ukulele slung over his shoulder has a sticker on it that reads THIS OBJECT DOES NOT EXIST.

"Is my scarf bothering you?" he asks in a surprisingly polite voice. A surprisingly nice voice for someone who had dubbed me Bad Karma. Auggie swings his scarf so it brushes back and forth against the top of my face on purpose. "Hola, Bad Karma? Are you awake?"

"No, Ugh-ie, and thanks for the scarf in my nose."

"Kewl," says Auggie, as if I'm completely serious. As if I actually like a scratchy wool scarf itching my nose. He's pulling his ukulele off his shoulder. He plucks at the strings for minute and then tucks it under his arm.

I want to stand up to my full height and overpower him. But this year, Auggie is almost as tall as me, so it won't work.

Glancing at his phone, he murmurs, "Niiiiiiiice," and starts to dance. His hips sway, his shoulders tilt, and his arms pivot back. Which means his ukulele clonks me on the head. "I got three hundred and nine LIKES in five minutes," he chants.

Three hundred and nine LIKES in five minutes? Really? *Really?*

Auggie just takes crazy random photos. He doesn't even care about what other people think. Or what filters are the most popular. He doesn't use inspiring quotes. He writes silly things such as *I like to blow bubbles in my chocolate milk.*

I shove a book aside in my locker and put some more away, getting what I need for my first few classes. At least Auggie hasn't started an eighth-grade Spirit Week Snappypic account. At least not one that I know about.

As I close my locker, Auggie spins on his heels, tilting his head the way my dog does when he's trying to understand something. "Bye, Karm."

Karm? Only my closest friends call me Karm.

Auggie's locker may be close to mine, but he is definitely not a friend.

I Hate Flippie!

During break after second period, Ella and I meet up by my locker. I ask her where she was earlier in the morning.

"At the orthodontist." She points to her mouth. "They went on a tightening rampage. I'm going to be so sore."

I pull out my flip phone and stare at it. "Flippie is so lame. Can I borrow yours for a second?"

She glances at her watch. We still have a few more minutes before the bell rings. She lowers her voice. "Be careful, okay?" She looks both ways for teachers.

I grab Ella's arm and we hustle away from the constant flow of students. Lots of them are saying hi. Renee Powell waves at me. She's an eighth grader who plays traveling soccer. She's one of the few girls at school who's taller than me.

"Can you help me get more followers?" Renee asks. "Seriously, we need to talk."

"Um, oh, sure. Maybe later?" I glance down at the

time on Ella's cell. I only have a few minutes now and I need to use my time wisely. I want to check out the seventh-grade Snappypic. Renee obviously has no idea that my account was cut off.

Renee salutes me. "Sure, okay." And she moves off down the hall to class.

Ella stands guard while I look at the seventh-grade Snappypic.

My fingers quickly scroll through everything. "Love the fonts you picked."

"Thanks." Ella smiles in her shy way.

"And the emojis." Ella put them next to a schedule of events for Spirit Week. "The dancing hot dog is the *best*." She posted a little hot dog guy that she drew in Merton colors, blue and gold. "All right!" I say, jumping up and down. "We're up to one hundred and eight followers!"

"That's great, Karm."

"Ha. There's no way Auggie can catch up."

I go into Ella's Snappypic. "Ella, if you want more followers, you really need to comment more on people's stuff," I say. "And you need to post things that look exciting. Or something cute. Or a photo where it looks like you're having the best time in the world."

"Okay," she says, but not very enthusiastically. She's heard all of this from me before. I LIKE a couple of super funny collages and I scroll through to Auggie's latest photo. It's not good. It's fuzzy. It's a close-up of his eyebrow. "Really? Everyone LIKES this?"

Ella freezes. "Put away my phone. There's a teacher." She points with her chin. "Coming right toward us."

I push the phone into my pocket.

"She didn't see. The halls are too crowded," I say as some girl's backpack practically bonks into my chin.

Ella glances at her watch again. "Karma, the bell's going to ring. You better give me back my phone."

"'Kay. Just one more thing."

"It's always one more thing," snaps Ella as she grabs her phone back. She hurries away.

Wow. Why is she suddenly all cranky?

For Real?

It's finally lunchtime. I'm standing just inside the cafeteria and I'm hearing a high-pitched squeal. "I-L-Y!"

It's Janel. She's waving over at Bailey to come sit down at the end of the table with her.

ILY stands for "I love you," and we use it all the time

on Snappypic. I mean, most of my followers did. And then I hear "I-L-Y" again over the din of other kids' voices, and it's Bailey. She's nodding right at me, her neat, chin-length hair bobbing. I nod back at her.

I've been ILYed plenty of times online for my photos on Snappypic, but in the middle of the Merton Middle School cafeteria by Bailey Jenners as I stand next to the spork, napkin, and fixins bar?

Nope, never.

"Get over here," says Bailey. "Remember, you're eating with us."

"Coming," I call out, smiling.

"So cool," Ella whispers under her breath.

The next thing I know, Ella and I are sitting with Bailey and the Bees. We're sitting by the Quik Cart, with its leopard spotty bananas and red apples that taste like Styrofoam. It's officially a lunchtime meeting of the chairs to plan Spirit Week.

Ella keeps bouncing in her chair and I send her a "keep calm" look. But of course I'm squishing my toes and clamping my teeth to keep from whooping out loud. Soon we all settle down and chat about this TV show and how crazy Mr. Derby the gym teacher is and how someone should fix the intercom.

"It's crazy. Not only is Spirit Week coming up, but this year the seventh grade is in charge of the dance," says Bailey. "But luckily, I have the best chairs ever for that." She nods at Janel and Megan. "So how's the snack situation for the dance going, people?"

"Excellent." Megan scoots in her chair as a couple boys squeeze past. "I posted on Google Docs a chart where PTA members can sign up to bring snacks."

"Fantastic," says Bailey, crunching on a cracker.

Megan smiles and pats her already-perfect ponytail. "And I've recruited fifteen girls to help put up the decorations in the gym. Yesterday I ordered the black paper to put up on the walls. Decorations are so handled. Except for the art part. That's Ella's job. Making the moons and stars. Stuff like that."

Ella takes a sip of her chocolate milk and grins at Megan.

"How's publicity going, Karma?" asks Bailey as she opens her salad tray.

I glance over at Ella. "Great. I made a Snappypic seventh-grade account. Ella designed it to look really cool. She put emojis next to everything. You know, like Crazy Hair Day and the hot dog–eating contest."

"I want to see," says Bailey. She hides her phone

in her lap, hops onto our page, and takes a bite of chicken salad. Megan and Janel lean in too. "Love, love, love the crazy pink hair you put next to Crazy Hair Day," says Bailey. "I totally want a pink beehive for Crazy Hair Day."

"I want to have alien hair," says Janel, "and put little wires in my hair so they look like antennae."

"Oh my gosh. We already have one hundred and eight followers!" says Bailey, looking at the seventh-grade page. "Karma, you're the best. Seriously." The girls at the next table turn to glance over at us.

"I still don't completely get how we're going to win and get the Spirit Stick thingy," says Megan.

Bailey sighs. "It's a numbers thing. We get points for each competition. Like which grade wins the hot dog–eating contest, or which grade has the most students who participate in Twin Day or wear school colors."

"There is someone seriously counting how many kids dress up with crazy hair and in blue and orange?" asks Ella.

Bailey fingers the scarf around her neck. "Of course. It's not arbitrary. The advisory teachers keep a tally and turn the numbers into Mrs. Grayson, who gives it to the principal." Bailey tucks her hair behind her ears.

"Thanks to Karma, I think we're going to win, people!"

Ella looks down at the table.

"And Ella," I add, feeling bad that everyone always forgets about her.

Snollygoster

As one of the custodians rumbles past, pushing his mop and broom cart to clean up a spill, Milton P. sets his shoe box down next to his sandwich. He's eating at a table with some kids everyone call the Aliens because they are so weird.

"There goes Snollygoster," says Megan. That was Auggie's nickname for Milton P. back in second grade, and it stuck like gum.

"That's mean, you guys," says Janel. "Remember, his dad died last spring. It can't be easy."

"That's so sad." Megan glances over at Milton P.'s table. "But c'mon, a shoe box?"

I sneak a look at him. "Yeah, that's a little weird." But as I say this I have this impulse. I'd love to photograph his shoe box and post this caption: *Anything could be inside.*

Cupping her hands around her mouth, Megan leans

into the group so her long, blond ponytail touches the table. For a moment, I worry for her. She doesn't look like the kind of person who would like crumbs in her hair. "In advisory, Mr. Jones made us go around the room and say stuff about ourselves. And then Milton P. said he's inventing a LEGO spaceship with levers and said it had some hyper something or other so it could transport cargo into the tenth dimension."

"Whoa, freaky," says Bailey.

"I think it's kind of cool," says Ella.

"Seriously?" Bailey nods over at Milton P., with his bangs plastered against his forehead, his semidarkened glasses, and his apple-red cheeks.

"No," Ella quickly says. "I was joking." But I have a feeling she isn't telling the truth.

The Truth

Later, during fifth period, when Ella and I sit together in French, I want to ask her about Milton P.

"*S'il vous plaît, la classe,* conjugate the verb of *being,*" says Madame Pessereau, pointing to the whiteboard where it says *Être*, which means "to be." She's wearing one of her many French pins, an Eiffel Tower, and beaming at us as if we can't wait to conjugate the verb of *being*. I bet Madame does it just for fun on the weekends.

I pull out my notebook and look at Ella. "So were you serious about Milton P. being cool?" I whisper.

"No," she says, but her face is pinkish. "Snollygoster? No way."

"Oh my gosh, you were serious, weren't you?"

She whispers into my ear. "He's not cool. He's extremely weird."

"Like he was programmed somewhere by an evil genius who wanted to play a joke?"

"Exactly. But he's, you know . . . still kinda, sorta cute."

"Because of his outer space eyes? And lashes a girl would kill for?"

"Yeah, but it's not just that. He's intriguing in a spy-like way," she says, her voice even lower. "But don't you dare tell anyone I said that." She flicks her gaze over at Bailey, who sits in the front row, conjugating away. "She and Janel and the rest of them would think that was *so* weird." The tips of Ella's ears blush.

"Wow, if only Milton P. knew."

Her eyes grow big. "Don't you dare, Karma Cooper!"

Madame Pessereau gives me a stern look, so I start copying what's on the board.

"No worries," I say out of the side of my mouth. "Because I don't think that Milton P. knows what girls are yet, even if he does know the secrets of the universe." Then I wink at her.

Sun streams in from the window and sort of winks too. Like the sun agrees.

Ella smiles and lets out a little sigh, and I think about what it feels like when you don't want people to know something about you. I'm glad that Ella feels as if she can trust me with secrets right here, in the middle of French class, conjugating *being*.

Polling

Hurrying to math, I ask Ella, "Can I see your phone?"

She bites her lip. "We're in the middle of the hall."

"I just want to check the seventh-grade Snappypic."

"Okay, be quick." She hands me her phone as we thread through the crowded hallway and pass by the seventh-grade science classrooms. The smell of formaldehyde and alcohol pierces the air. I hate asking Ella's permission every time. I know it makes her nervous.

I check the hall for any signs of a teacher. The hallway is full of kids, a few of them even checking their phones. And now I'm doing the same. "So cool, Ella. The background you used looks like rainbow confetti."

Fidgeting with the buttons on her top, Ella steps aside for a teacher in a rush to get by. I quickly hide the phone out of sight.

"Maybe I could blow up some of the drawings and put them up at the dance," says Ella. "For decorations. Megan wanted me to help. "

I pause and try to figure out how to say this. Ella's drawings are always a little, well, quirky. Some people might even say weird. She might give someone blue hair, or someone else might have cat ears. A table could have feet with running shoes. I lean in toward Ella and huff, "Megan wants the decorations to go with the theme, stars and moons. You know her, picky. Just make them plain."

Ella blushes. "Well, I kind of already made the stars and moons during fifth period with an app I have on my phone. I even put them on Google Drive. I guess I got excited."

"Let me see."

She shows me. And I try not to frown. The moons have sunglasses and the stars have oddly shaped noses, ears, and lips. "Wow. Those are really creative. But I think Megan wanted regular-looking stars and moons. That's what everyone likes."

"Really?" Ella looks disappointed.

I nod.

"Okay. I can make regular ones too."

"Great. Perfect." I breathe out a sigh of relief.

A bunch of girls with flute cases hurry past us in the opposite direction. I feel a little bad, but I'd hate for Ella to get shot down in front of the Bees. I try to make my voice sound light. "You know I love your sketches. Whatever you do will be awesome. Megan already ordered black paper to line the walls, so the decorations will pop at the dance."

A slight smile grows on Ella's face as we turn down the hallway. A walkie-talkie crackles down the hall in back of us and students snap their phones shut.

A kid whispers, "It's the principal."

I immediately push Ella's phone into my pocket. The principal, Mrs. Wallace, heads toward me. She's walking with an older woman with short black hair.

She's staring right at me. Did she see the phone? Ella shoots me an extra-worried look. Kids nearby all gape at us. I can't get one more detention, or else it's Club Suspension for me.

My heart hammers in my chest as Mrs. Wallace nods at me. My insides chill.

"Nice to see you, Miss Cooper," she says. "I understand you and Ella are doing wonderful things for your Spirit committee."

"Thanks," I say, feeling a huge relief she didn't see the rogue phone.

Something Should Be Done About Ceilings

When I get home from school, there's a note from Mom taped to the fridge. She'll be home early-ish today. But first she's picking Toby up from aftercare at school, and she wants me to take out the chicken. She writes:

Please remember this time ☺

After I pull the chicken thighs out of the freezer, I go up to my room and yank my homework assignments, notebooks, and textbooks out of my backpack. My Hebrew homework sits on my desk. Tomorrow after school I go to Maxine, my Hebrew tutor, to help me prepare for my bat mitzvah. I flop onto my bed and stare at the ceiling. Somehow I'm also supposed to figure out a service project for my bat mitzvah. That means doing some kind of good deed. I have no idea what to do. It's a little overwhelming.

Lucky hangs out with me on the floor with his doggie chew toy. He puts his chin between his paws. He seems bored too.

I stare at the ceiling and realize just how boring ceilings can be.

Unless I took a photo of it and used a really cool filter. Maybe rainbow effects.

Then I hear Mom's car pulling into the driveway. The front door opens and Mom calls out, "Hi, Karma. We're home!"

"Hi," I yell down. I stare at my books spread out on the floor.

"Did you take out the chicken?"

"Yes."

"Want to cook with me?"

"No thanks," I call down.

Mom suddenly bursts into my room. Her eyes look big and excited. "So I figured out what you can do for your community service project for your bat mitzvah. You can volunteer at the historical society."

"The what? No. That sounds boring."

"Look. Just give it a try. They keep all kinds of old

photos there. I spoke with Neda Grubner about you. She said you could do some filing and sorting. And she said that you could—"

"Mom. I'll figure something out."

"You've had plenty of time for that. Your bat mitzvah is coming up in a few months. There isn't time. That's why you're going to the historical society after school now."

"Really? Now?"

"Yes, Karma. Just try."

Toby tromps up the stairs and pokes his head into my room. "Want to play?"

"No." My knee bounces up and down like a yo-yo.

"I can't." Nobody else has to go to a historical society right after school. Everyone else gets to relax. It's so unfair. I was in school all day long. I have a headache.

Toby darts into the hallway. He tosses his soccer ball into the air. "Will you kick with me, Karma?"

"Not now, Toby. I've got to do something. I've got to go somewhere with Mom. For my community service project."

"You make it sound all important," says Toby.

"It is," I say, although I don't really believe it.

My Stats:

309 LIKES for Auggie's photo of chocolate milk. Really?

1 principal who did not catch me on Ella's phone. Yay!

108 followers of the seventh-grade Snappypic account

1 community service project after school at a history place. Really?

1 BFF who thinks Milton P. the shoe box boy is secretly cute. Which makes me think that maybe, just maybe, if Auggie wasn't Auggie, he could be sort of cute too.

Mood: A little annoyed—Mom is being so controlling with this community service thing!

8

It's Historic (and Therefore Doomed to Be Boring)

Mom drops me off at the historical society. It's an old-fashioned–looking Victorian house with a plaque in front saying it's a historic building, as if that wasn't obvious. I trudge up the stairs. How did I agree to this? If I told anyone about it, they'd think it was the most boring thing ever. For Talia's project, she's working with the Humane Society. Everyone loves the photos she posts on Snappypic of the new kittens. Last week she posted these kitties that looked like Oreo cookies. I wanted to eat them up!

And even Milton P.'s project was cool. He built a

LEGO replica of the courthouse, and it's on display at the library. He got a lot of high-fives for that. But filing? I'm yawning already. Filing sounds like something you do to your nails, or do to your teeth if you are a bad guy, or that people pay real clerks and secretaries to do.

I ring a bell. The door buzzes and I walk into a small lobby. One wall has a glass display case. Inside of it a banner reads CELEBRATING HISTORY! It's full of old-looking household items like irons and a washing board. And then next to the display case there's a slideshow playing on the wall, with old-looking photographs of people and buildings.

I shuffle over to a counter, where a silver-haired guard sits. All this security surprises me. It's not like the historical society is a jewelry store with diamonds and rubies. Once I give the guard my name and explain I'm a volunteer, he nods and waves me through. I step into a huge room with ceilings, but there's nobody there. Not that I was expecting a welcome party. There are three desks and a couple computers. A "Happy Birthday" helium balloon half floats and half sags over a desk chair.

I drift through the room and take an old oak staircase to the second floor. A musty, woody, papery smell tickles my nose.

Upstairs a young woman dressed in a black cable-knit sweater sits behind a large circulation-type desk, like you'd see at a library, only this one is filled with stacks of papers and boxes.

"You must be Karma," she says with a smile. "I'm Anna Eng, head researcher and archivist for the historical society." We shake hands.

Anna wears dark glasses that tip up into little points. They make her look slightly mysterious and cool. She's got on brightly colored stockings that look almost like an abstract photographic image. It's as though she's wearing art.

"So, welcome to the historical society," Anna says cheerfully. "Today we're down a couple of volunteers because of illnesses." She motions to a part of the room that is part library and part office, full of books and filing cabinets. A couple of older women sit at tables, reading files. One of them glances up and smiles. The other doesn't seem to notice me at all.

"The executive director will meet with you for your intake," Anna continues. She nods at a silver-haired woman in the very back reaching for some sort of box.

"Okay," I say. The intake? Wow. It sounds so official.

The silver-haired woman whirls around. The

executive director is, of course, Neda Grubner. Won-derful. Of course, Mom did warn me. Neda puts a box down on a table and clomps toward me in her high heels. She also wears black eyeglasses, but hers are huge ovals. I guess black eyeglasses are a thing around here.

"I'm so glad you decided to meet us today," says Neda. She purses her trout lips. She doesn't shake my hand. "We don't get too many middle-school student volunteers." She glances at Anna significantly. "We usu-ally take in master's degree candidates or undergraduates, occasionally mature high school students." She empha-sizes *mature*. And suddenly I'm feeling like a preschooler with ice cream dripping down my chin.

"So you are our very first," says Anna, holding up her pointer finger. I think that's a compliment, so I smile back at her.

"We'll go back downstairs." Neda points to the oak stairs.

Together, we go back down the stairs. Neda sits at the desk, the one with the limp balloon.

"What exactly is an intake?" I guess if I were *mature* I would know the answer already.

Neda pulls off her glasses and twirls them. "It's to find out a little about your interests. In terms of history."

She sighs heavily. What if I told her that I didn't have any interests in terms of history? That it was my mom's suggestion?

Putting her owlish glasses back on, Neda starts to ask me about my interests. I tell her about how I like to take pictures. And how a lot of people really like my photos. I tell her I've taken thousands of shots. Her owly eyes get even bigger when I tell her that. I don't tell her that my Snappypic account doesn't exist anymore and that I can't ever look at my photos and the comments and the LIKES.

"Photography is one of the most powerful forms of historic documentation," explores Neda in a lecture-y voice.

"Yeah. You can capture a moment. And share it," I say.

"Have you ever taken a photography class?"

I shake my head.

Neda puckers her mouth. Her lipstick is very orange-y. "Can I be honest with you, Karma?"

Am I supposed to say no? Whenever someone starts anything with "to be honest" or "not to be insulting," you know it's going to be bad and insulting.

Neda scoots closer. She clears her throat. "Like

Anna said, we've never taken in anyone so young before. The documents and photos that we handle can be very delicate. Many are over a hundred years old and are often one of a kind. We have to be very careful. We have a responsibility as curators for the community. It can be busy around here. We respond to research inquiries of all kinds, so when we take on someone as young as yourself, well, to be frank, it gives me pause. I told your mother I'd meet with you and that we'd see. You can volunteer here, but on a trial basis."

What? A trial? This makes it sound like I'm a criminal. I stare at the half-inflated balloon. I wonder when it will fall. It doesn't have much life left in it.

"I hope this isn't coming as a surprise to you," says Neda.

"No," I lie.

She's twirling her glasses again. "I worry that someone your age won't have the . . . uh, maturity."

"I'm very mature for my age!" I spurt out. "I'm the tallest girl in my class, almost. And it's not like I'm going to crayon on anything. I can do this," I say with determination.

Neda lets out a deep breath and studies me. "I see

you'd really like to do this." Well, that's a good start. Her telling me that I couldn't do it makes me want to prove her wrong.

"I can do this for sure," I say.

"Let's try each other out, then. Your mother tells me that you need about twenty hours of service." She peers at a calendar on her desk. "That means if you come twice a week for about three weeks, you'd be good. That would put Thursday, March 22 as your stop date."

"Sounds good," I say.

Neda pushes her glasses down her nose and peers at me intently. "Would you be interested in helping to write up grants? Oh, forget that question. We're going to skip over to the bottom here." The bottom would be her list of intake questions, I guess. Maybe I've passed some sort of test. I think, suddenly, I'm feeling almost excited.

"Are you good with computers?"

"Really good."

"Copy machines? Printers?"

I nod. "Well, yeah, I'm good at fixing the printer when it jams at our house."

She clicks her long nails on the table. "And do you have a favorite time period?" Neda scoots even closer to me, as if that might jog my brain. "The 1840s? The 1890s? World War I?"

"Um, well. Nothing really in particular," I say. "It's all interesting."

"Fine. Noted." She runs something down on her pad. "Well, from the sounds of things, you're an excellent photographer. And that's an area where we could use a lot of help."

"Great," I say, and suddenly my heart is pounding. For some reason, I didn't think a historical society would have a lot of photos, but it makes sense, of course, that it would.

"Listen, I've got a meeting with the fund-raising committee soon." She glances at her watch. "So I'll expect you back here on Thursday afternoon. Will that work for your schedule?"

"I'm pretty sure. I'll check with my mom. But I think so."

"Good." And for the first time, Neda almost smiles.

And I sort of smile back at her.

"We'll look forward to seeing you on Thursday, then," she says. "You'll get a tour, and we'll put you to work."

"I'm looking forward to it," I say, and maybe this time I'm not lying.

My Stats:

0 interest in filing old papers

2 pairs of black glasses observed

1 half-dead birthday balloon observed and un-popped

1 person with orange-y lipstick who I want to prove is wrong about me being immature

1 new volunteer community service job that is on a trial basis

Mood: Mad that I have to try out to volunteer!

9

Advisory Ruin

In advisory, I realize that I have forgotten to give Ella back her phone. I had borrowed it right before school when I was complaining to her about the historical society. Oh well, might as well take full advantage of having it. Suddenly, an announcement from Principal Wallace comes over the PA about Spirit Week:

"Merton Dolphins, get ready for some Spirit Week fun. Monday, March 19 will be Crazy Hair Day! Don't forget to bring a can of food for people in need! Tuesday, March 20 will be the hot dog–eating contest! Wednesday, March 21 will be Twin

Day! The last day for the canned food drive will be Thursday, March 22. And Friday, March 23 will be School Color Day and the Spirit Rally. The Spirit Week dance will be after school that day at 6:30 p.m. in the gym. Go, Dolphins!"

Oh, that gives me an idea. Ella and I should definitely post a lot of reminders about this to the seventh-grade Spirit Week followers. I peek at Auggie's eighth-grade Spirit page by propping up my math book as a shield from Mr. Chase's eyes. My heart beats quickly as the rain hammers on the roof of the school. Mr. Chase strides down the aisle toward me. I close my book shut. He stands against the back wall of the classroom where he shifts around some stacks of books on a shelf. Does he suspect something?

No, Mr. Chase is striding past my seat again, back to his desk. He would have said something. I prop up my book and glance at my phone. Unfortunately, Auggie just told his Snappypic followers to follow his new eighth-grade Spirit Week page.

His Spirit Week page now has 602 followers. I let out an "eep" and my math book clunks onto the floor.

From behind his desk, Mr. Chase shoots me a stern look, and not because of the book falling.

He has seen the phone. He slaps his big hands against the desktop. A paper drifts down onto the floor.

Uh-oh.

Mr. Chase waves a yellow pencil, which appears small in his massive, clumpy hands. "This is a warning, Karma Cooper. I don't want to see you with your phone out *ever* again, even if you do have hundreds of followers."

Huge relief. Just a warning and not a detention. He glares at me, clears his throat, and then addresses the entire advisory. "Apparently, some people think the rules don't apply to them. Some people need to hear the rules regarding cell phone usage at school. Again."

Then Mr. Chase stands up to his full height and reads all the rules. Again. The one that he reads the loudest is this: There's a new policy that if you get caught with a phone in class, they lock it up in the office like it's in prison.

Mr. Chase thumps on his desk to get our attention. "So people, cell phones are not to be seen or heard. And if you're carrying one, do yourself a favor and put it on silent. And do not pull it out in my presence." He locks eyes with me. "Got it, Miss Cooper?"

"Got it."

Why did I forget to give Ella her phone? If I had remembered, this never would have happened. Now he's onto me.

Weird

During lunch, Ella sits down next to me eating her couscous salad, and I'm crunching on my chicken taco. When I give her the phone back, I don't tell her about almost getting caught by Mr. Chase.

We're eating with Bailey and the Bees again. Bailey sits across from me eating a tuna sandwich. She's flirting with a bunch of cute boys who drift by the table to annoy us. Half the cafeteria keeps on glancing our way. Ella and I can't stop grinning at each other. After the boys leave, some girls swarm over to say hi to the Bees.

They throw out compliments like "love your shirt." Or "Did you do something to your hair?" But the crazy thing is, they are also doing it to Ella.

I wink at her.

And she winks back. It's like we've finally arrived at this tropical resort vacation we've only just dreamed about and now we're surfing the biggest and best wave ever.

Then Bailey reminds us about the Spirit Week meeting after school at her house at 4:30 p.m. tomorrow. "Don't worry," I say. "There's no way I'll forget."

Then suddenly, Milton P. shuffles over toward the table. He's holding his shoe box under his left arm, and in his right hand he grips a blue lunch sack. Ella's mouth falls open. Her breath catches in her throat.

"Oh my gosh," says Janel as she opens her drink and takes a sip.

Megan taps Bailey on the shoulder. Both of them scrunch their eyebrows in confusion.

I can't blame them.

My first instinct is to duck. Milton P. is waving at us as he gets closer, like we're his long-lost sisters.

I don't want to be mean, so I wave back and so does Ella, but she hisses under her breath, "You told him I thought he was cute!"

"No. Promise."

"I'm going to kill you, Karma Cooper."

"I seriously didn't say a thing!"

The entire caf is looking at him looking at all of us. But then this little thought comes to me. Somehow Milton P. Daniels must have special abilities. He claims to build spaceships. What if he has real powers of some kind? What if he can read minds? And then another thought zaps me. Back in elementary school, both Milton P. and I were teased. Even though we didn't hang out, we knew we were the same. Outsiders. And not well liked.

As Milton P. steps toward our table, I squint and try to figure out how Ella can see his cuteness. A thick brown belt holds up his too-baggy jeans. The busy checked pattern on his shirt makes me dizzy. But I almost glimpse it for a second, if you take away the shoe box clutched under his arm, his strange robotic shuffle, and his bangs plastered against his forehead. Maybe, possibly.

"I swear I didn't say anything," I whisper to Ella. "You have to believe me."

"Why is he coming toward us, then?"

But he doesn't stop in front of Ella.

Are You Kidding Me?

Here's the weird thing. Milton P. Daniels stops in front of me, Karma Cooper.

And he smiles at me with his outer-space eyes while his mouth stretches in a little line, expressionless. And then, as he clutches his shoe box in the middle of the cafeteria, with everyone's ears turned our way, he says in his robot-y voice, "Karma Cooper, I always knew you'd appreciate red aircraft fuselage curved aft section six by ten bottom with fire logo pattern on both sides."

"Huh?" I say as everyone stares.

Because it's Milton P. and he's talking to me. And nobody has any idea what he just said.

I choke back a laugh. "Sure," I say. "Whatever."

"See you later." Milton P.'s neck pivots down, as if there's a rod inside of it, as if he's really made of steel and not flesh. A hint of a smile tugs at his lips. Then he tucks his shoe box under his left arm and plods away.

Ella sits next to me, blinking in surprise. As Milton P. marches across the cafeteria, there are snorts of laughter as someone calls out, "What do you got in there, Snollygoster? Someone's head?"

"His box is from outer space. He's communicating with his mother ship!" cracks a kid sitting behind me in a hockey shirt. I think it's Brian Feeker.

There's a burst of laughter. But Milton P. doesn't react. My throat feels dry. I can't help feeling badly. I stare outside the window, where a steady rain beats down.

Milton P. plods across the cafeteria as if his legs don't have joints, then sits down to eat his lunch.

"Um, people, what was that about?" asks Bailey, pressing her lips together.

I shrug. "No clue."

And it's true.

I don't have a clue.

And I don't want to know.

My Stats:

No new followers on the seventh-grade Spirit Week page

602 followers on Auggie's eighth-grade Spirit Week page—argh!

1 warning by Mr. Chase—but not a detention! YAY!

1 mysterious utterance by Milton P. Daniels. No idea why he decided to speak to me after all this time.

Mood: Baffled and hopeful that Milton P. lunchroom encounter is an isolated incident

10

> Wag More

After I get home from Hebrew tutoring, I fling my backpack and soccer bag into the front hallway. Lucky noses into me and I scratch him behind his ears. His tail swishes back and forth.

Dad pokes his head into the hall. "How was Hebrew?"

"Fine." I rub under Lucky's chin.

"Hey, Lucky, you're such a cutie," says Dad. "Yes, you are. You're *so* cute."

Lucky's golden-brown tail swishes faster. It looks like a flame. I could take such a cool photo. I'd get so many LIKES with that. People love dog shots. "I want to take a photo so badly, but I can't."

Dad puts his arm on my shoulder. "Look, I'm not giving you back your phone, but I have idea." He strolls over to the cabinet in the den. "I got this five years ago." He pulls out a digital camera. "It's just sitting here gathering dust. It's a good one. Why don't you use it?"

I peer at the camera. I have no idea how to work it. There are so many buttons. "Maybe," I say.

"Yay! Karma's home!" Suddenly Toby is pounding halfway down the stairs. "Want to see what I built?"

Closing my eyes, I think about the science lab report I have to write up and the social studies questions and math I have to do, even though I'm beat from doing all of that Hebrew. Oh, and I have to do a summary of a short story for language arts. Summaries are so stupid. I mean, it's a short story. That's why it's short, so you can read it quickly. I always, always have Floyd next to me when I do my homework.

Ugh.

I glance up as Toby thumps partway down the stairs. "Want to see what I made?" he asks again.

"Can you answer your brother?" Dad strolls all the

way into the hallway, sits on the bench beside the shoe basket, and scoops out his loafers.

"Can't. I've got homework in four subjects. Oh yeah, and studying for Hebrew too."

I pull out my folder with my Hebrew in it. It's *Shemot*, the first book of *Exodus*. That's the part I'm going to read and discuss for my bat mitzvah. It's when Moses flees Egypt and goes to Midian. He's in trouble and has to leave everything behind. He basically says he's a stranger in a strange land. No friends. No family. No more prince of Egypt. My eyes gaze at the Hebrew letters. I know how to pronounce them, but I don't know what more I could say about Moses in front of hundreds of people.

Sometimes I feel that, in general, I know how to say things but I have no idea what anything means.

Feeling Peace

After dinner Mom has a work meeting, so Dad bikes with Toby and me to Salt & Straw, our favorite ice cream shop, which has really awesome and wild flavors. I get strawberry with cilantro lime cheesecake. Toby picks sea salt ice cream with a caramel ribbon, and Dad chooses goat cheese marionberry habenero. We're sitting down at a little wooden table and Dad takes a photo of us holding our cones. He starts to send it to Mom when his phone rings.

"It's your mother." Dad glances down at the screen. "How do I not lose what I have and answer the call?"

Toby leans across the table. "I'll show you." He grabs the phone and starts talking to Mom.

Dad throws up his hands, laughing. "Okay, guess I'm officially clueless. My second grader knows more than me."

I nudge Dad with my elbow. "Toby does know more."

Suddenly Dad gets a sly look on his face. "So tell me about this boy."

"A boy?"

"Yes, I've heard you talking about him."

"What boy? What are you talking about?"

"On the phone with Ella. I've heard you many times. Discussing a crush."

"Do you mean Auggie? Puh-lease. Because he's more like my archenemy."

Dad shakes his head. "Nope. His name start with an *F*." He snaps his fingers. "Floyd. That's it. When I picked you up from school, I overheard you say how much you like him, and miss him, and . . ."

Then my brother and I start laughing so hard we practically hyperventilate.

Dad shrugs. "What? I know I'm clueless, but you've got to tell me what's so funny."

"Floyd is Karma's phone," says Toby, who's clutching his stomach because he's laughing so hard.

My Stats:
? followers on the seventh-grade Spirit Week page. Don't know cause I can't check.
? followers on Auggie's eighth-grade Spirit Week page. Ditto.
1 awesome ice cream cone devoured
1 almost-boyfriend named Floyd

Mood: Kind of silly

11

Retainer Kind of Day

Naturally, I pass by Auggie Elson in the corridor right next to the bulletin board with the "How to Help a Choking Victim" poster.

Auggie sings my name. "Hey, Karma Karma Karma. How's the canned food drive coming?"

I reply, "Good," only I just mouth the word because I don't want Auggie to stop and actually talk to me when I still have my retainer in my mouth. I forgot to take it out before I went to school. I only have to wear my retainer at night. I need to spit it out ASAP!

Wait a minute. It's weird to care what I look like

since it's Auggie. But still, other people might see. I whip around to face the wall, yank out my retainer, and stuff it into the front pocket of my backpack.

"Nice retainer!" calls out Auggie as he struts down the hall backward. My face is blow-dryer hot now.

In my mind, I text, *I wish I had a hoodie on right now so I could block Auggie from view.*

If I had my Snappypic, I'd make sure to make a sarcastic comment on one of his photo bombs. But I don't. I have a slimy retainer in my backpack.

Why

The last bell rings and Ella and I file out of the library. Mr. Schlesinger, our science teacher, brought our class there to do research for our reports on cell development. We reach the double doors of the cafeteria in two minutes.

"Should we go in?" asks Ella. She glances at a clock on the wall. "It's so early."

I shrug. "Let's do it." We've never gone immediately from third period before. Normally we'd go to our lockers, but they're way across school. The minute we go through the double doors, I know it's a mistake. Less than a dozen kids mill around inside. Most of the round tables sit empty, and there's only one person on the hot lunch line. Bailey and the Bees are not yet at their table by the Quick Cart. Of course nobody—*nobody*—at Merton will sit at that spot. Even though there's not a RESERVED sign there, there might as well be.

"Should we sit down at their table?" asks Ella, as we stand alone near the front entrance.

"Yeah, sure. Why not?"

"But it'd be weird. Right?" She peeps at the table.

"No, we've been eating with them for a while." I try to sound convincing. So we sit at Bailey's table.

Some boys call out to their friends by the entrance and I turn to look. Bailey and the Bees are strolling in now.

They're here.

I nudge Ella's side. "It's them."

She stares ahead with huge eyes, like Lucky does when he's caught with people food in his mouth.

"Don't stare," I hiss.

"I'm not. I'm checking out my nail polish."

"Yeah right." The Bees are all dressed in skinny jeans, bright tops, and cute flats. Megan has her honey-blond hair pulled back into a tight ponytail, while Bailey and Janel wear their hair down.

Bailey waves at us as she nears the table. "Sorry we're late," she says. And that's it. Not "What are you doing sitting here?" This is my reality. Remember it. Like a snapshot.

The Table of Tables

We go to sit down with Bailey and the Bees, and I'm smiling so big. They sit at a round table with six seats. "Ella, I like that color top," says Janel. "Lemon-yellow looks awesome on you."

Bailey glances at my homemade gluten-free pizza. "Wow, does your mom have a cooking show? What's on your pizza?"

"Sliced olives and morel mushrooms," I say as I dig in.

Ella opens her chicken salad sandwich. "Her mom makes her all this creative stuff. It's supercrazy."

We start talking about the weirdest food our mothers have packed for us. The mention of weird things leads to us talking about Milton P. Daniels. Today his shoe box is wrapped in silver duct tape, the shiny kind that gleams under the lights.

As I shift in my chair to glance over at Milton P., he catches my eye. His hands *thwack* onto the roof of the taco fixing bar. "Karma, remember, your storage drawers need to be opaque!" he calls out. "Or else they are useless."

"Okaaaaay." My face burns as his eyes laser in on me. I pivot back around.

Everyone giggles, covering their mouths.

Bailey cocks her head to the side and presses her lips together like she's going to button them. "Now that was different." Megan nods in agreement, and Ella nervously looks down at her ink-stained art hands.

"Yeah, tell me about it." I shake my carton of milk. "I seriously have no idea what that was about."

"Pure Milton P." Janel stirs her yogurt. "He arrived here from his own planet."

"Just what is in that shoe box thingy, anyway?" asks Megan.

"Bones," says Janel. "Of his pet guinea pig or something."

"I'm thinking dozens of chocolate bars," says Bailey. "He is on the hefty side."

"Maybe a secret transmitter," says Ella. "Since he's a spy." We all laugh.

Swirling her milk carton, Bailey squints at Milton P. as if she's trying to figure something out. "I don't get why Milton P. talks to you."

"Or what he means when he does," says Janel.

"Me either." I pull a pear out of my lunch bag. Okay, that's not true. But I just can't say. Ella gives me a worried look. We both know why Milton P. might feel bonded to me.

In fourth grade, Milton P. sat by himself next to the globe of the world. I sat by myself next to the sink in the back of the room.

We were both outcasts.

But I just can't say that to Bailey and the Bees. They didn't really know the old me. Bailey knew me, of course, but she doesn't seem to remember. Thank you, thank you, thank you.

In my mind, I text, *Why does Milton P. bother with me now all of a sudden? I don't get it. But I'm not sure I want to find out.*

Free

I'm at home in my room getting ready to bike to the historical society. I need to go in twenty minutes. A photocopy of my Torah portion sits on the corner of my desk. That's the part I'm going to read from the Hebrew Bible. I still have no idea what I'm going to say about it for my *drosh*, which is a teaching lesson you have to give during your bat mitzvah about your Torah portion. I guess I'm supposed to be philosophical or something.

I can be a philosopher. I text in my mind, *I am bored. Because I am.*

Yeah, I'm actually listening to the heater. I didn't realize how much noise a heater makes—a rushing sound, like wind that is constant and regular and then slows down as if it's a little tired, like it needs a break, just like me.

And without thinking, I finally look at my Torah portion. I'm surprised how easily the words slip off my tongue, almost as if I've been storing them there and they've been waiting to be free.

My Stats:
3 Bees who seem to be friends
1 kid who may be from outer space who doesn't stop talking to me
1 Torah portion that maybe I actually know
1 community service volunteer job where I need to show someone with orange lips that I'm mature!

Mood: Kind of looking forward to proving the person with orange lips wrong!

12

The Hysterical Society

So I'm at the historical society. I have my notebook and the pen I swiped from my dad's desk. I'm even wearing a skirt. Before I left, Toby kept on telling me I looked too serious for the Hysterical Society and cracked himself up. This time I ride my bike there, which was probably not the best idea in a skirt.

When I buzz myself into the large bottom floor, the little balloon is gone. Officially deflated, I guess. Neda sits at her desk, working on the computer. She glances up, and for a moment she looks almost surprised to see me, her lips dropping down into her trout pucker, but then her head pops back to her screen. I get the feeling that she's really not that busy but likes to look busy. Mom says I do that too when she wants me to do a chore.

Out of the corner of her eye, Neda watches me climb up the oak staircase. It makes me feel all suspicious. *Sorry, but I'm not a criminal. I'm a volunteer! And I'm going to be the best one ever, even though I'm in middle school.* But Anna, the researcher, isn't like that. She smiles when she sees me. She's wearing a black top again. But her skirt is an awesome lime-green plaid. "Ready?" she asks.

"Yup," I say.

She hops out of her desk chair. "It's been a busy, crazy day. So many rush research requests. Only just finished lunch now."

"Wow." I look up at the clock over her desk. It's already 3:30. I have a Spirit Week meeting with Bailey and the Bees at 4:45, so I'm going to try to sneak out of here in an hour without Neda seeing.

"So let me introduce you to some of our volunteers."

Anna points to a fifty-something woman on a computer. "That's Karen. She's newer. And is working on a request." Karen gives me a half wave. She wears little earrings with bananas on them. I guess fruit jewelry is a trend at the historical society.

"Karen's a recently retired school librarian," explains Anna. "But I'm not sure about the retired. She's putting in some good hours around here."

Karen glances up from the file folder on her lap. "I can't help myself."

Anna laughs. She strolls over to a wooden table to the left of the circulation desk and I follow her. "Karma, this is Dorina. She's been a volunteer for eleven years and pretty much owns the place."

"Oh, I don't know about that," says Dorina. She's got one of those teased-up hairdos that is shaped like an upside-down artichoke.

"So today Dorina will be showing you around," says Anna.

Dorina smiles at me and I see that she's wearing feather earrings and a teal sweater vest.

"Teal is my favorite color," I say.

"It's my second favorite," says Dorina. "Purple is my number one."

I wonder if Neda has told her that I'm here on a trial basis. My legs start to bounce. They bounce harder when I think about how I have to sneak out of here without being seen since I'm supposed to be at the Spirit Week meeting at 4:45, and I'm supposed to stay here until 5:00.

I whip out my little spiral notebook.

"My, I can see you're nice and prepared." Dorina then shows me around, pointing out the different aisles and what's in each one. It really does look a lot like a library, only messier, with more boxes and rolled-up maps and stuff.

Dorina gestures at the back wall, where there are all kinds of shelves. "There are your ephemera boxes, and over there we have—"

"Ephemera." I like that word, even though I have no idea what it means. If I had Floyd I could look it up right away.

"Yes," she says. "The index for them is over here. So the *As* start on the left back wall and then there you have the *Zs* on the back right. It's where we keep the paper things. Newspaper clippings, brochures. No photos. It's all archival quality to keep it from turning yellow. If you want to go through them, wear the gloves." She points to a table where there are boxes of them.

I scribble as much as I can into my notebook. I peep up at the clock. I have to leave in forty minutes. Yikes.

"You don't think there's going to be a test, do you?" Dorina says, laughing. "Because just when you think you know where everything goes, they'll do a reorganization around here just to mess with you."

"Thanks for the warning."

Next we walk over to another aisle and Dorina pulls out a thick binder. "This is one of my go-to spots. It's a listing of buildings by city and street address."

I nod, although I have no idea why you would need something like that.

"That's a lot," I say. I mean everything. Not just the binder.

She laughs. "This isn't even half of it, honey. So why don't you spend some time just sniffing around, getting used to what goes where. Just remember to put everything back exactly where you found it."

I give a salute. "Will do!"

I spend time just being a general snoop. I'm peeking into another file when Karen rushes up to Dorina. They talk excitedly about something, and then Dorina whips out some binders.

"Aha!" says Dorina triumphantly.

Anna and I trot over to find out exactly what's going on.

Karen explains that a woman from Texas claimed that her great-grandfather was born here in the county, but when they went for a family vacation and searched for his house, all they found was a grassy field. She thought he might have forgotten the right address or that maybe he wasn't from around here at all.

"But I had a hunch and dug up some records." Karen waves a Xeroxed piece of paper. "And I discovered that the woman's great-grandfather, Ivan McMurphy, was an orphan." She pulls a photo out of her file. "See. This is Ivan when he was a baby."

I study the black-and-white photo. Well, it's more brownish. Ivan has big, blond curls and a mischievous grin. "There're no details here to tell you where this was taken," I point out.

"Exactly," says Karen.

Dorina's smile now grows extra big. "So I looked at the organizational index and saw that the old orphanage was knocked down. And low and behold, I checked my listing file, and the address matched. Ivan was born in the orphanage!"

It's sort of amazing, but all those files and boxes mean something. They work.

"Good job, ladies." Anna claps her hands. "A perfect end to a crazy day."

"Wow," I say. "You used all of that"—I wave my

hands at all the collected pieces of the past—"to solve a mystery."

"Exactly," says Karen. "That's why I love this place."

I peer at the photo of the orphanage. "Hey, it looks like the photographer cut off part of the building."

Anna takes a closer look. "You're right. You've got good eyes, Karma."

"Thanks," I say.

Glancing up from the photo, Anna smiles at me. "Have you ever taken a photography class?"

I shake my head. Why is everyone around here asking me that?

"You should. There's a volunteer, Katherine, who works here. She was just telling me her son is teaching one at the community rec center. You should sign up."

"Is it for"—I pause—"kids?" I'm afraid of Neda overhearing. If she thought there was a bona fide kid in here, she'd probably have a fit.

"Teens, I think. But if you're twelve you can do it."

It's weird thinking of myself as old enough to take a class for teens, but then again, I'm almost thirteen and ready to be bat mitzvahed.

"From what I understand," says Dorina, "he's a really great instructor. He teaches one for older adults as well."

Anna looks back at me as she strolls to her desk. "I think you'd enjoy it."

"Maybe," I say.

> ## Click

The first thing I do when I get home is take Dad's camera out of the cabinet in the family room. What would it be like to take a photography class? How different can it be? I pull the camera out of the case. It feels so much heavier than Floyd. It's got a big lens that looks professional.

I take out the little instruction booklet and flip through it, reading the names of all the parts. Shutter release. Hot shoe for flash. Red-eye reduction light. Optical viewfinder. Lens barrel. So much stuff and that's not even half of it. When I turn on the camera, it makes a satisfying whirring noise as if it's happy. I push down on the button you use to take a picture, which I now know is called the shutter release.

Click. I take a photo of my hand.

Click. And the floor.

Click. And my dresser.

The camera works.

I pick up the instructions to read more when Mom

calls my name. With the camera slung over my shoulder, I pad over to the kitchen. Mom is chopping up romaine lettuce for the salad. She asks me how it went at the historical society.

"It's weird," I confess, "but the time went superfast."

"That's great, Karma." She rinses the leaves in the spinner. Toby's in the next room building his LEGOs. Her eyes graze my shoulder. "I see you've discovered Dad's camera."

"Yup," I say.

"Hey," calls out Toby, "I heard you say something was weird."

"I thought the historical society would be full of spiderwebs, but it was actually kind of cool." I explain how together Karen and Dorina solved a family mystery.

Later I go into Dad's office and look up the word *ephemera*. It means something fleeting. Something enjoyed for a little while. Ephemera are also collected items, usually printed, that were supposed to be useful for a short time. I think about the boxes in the historical society. They preserve something that was supposed to be temporary, and it makes me think: *If I could only pick a few items to box up and preserve forever, what would they be?*

And then something hits me.

Something really bad.

I completely forgot about the Spirit Week meeting. Immediately I reach for my phone. Of course I can't text on my poor Flippie. I'll have to call. I hope nobody is too mad. Somehow, with all the excitement of finding out about the orphan guy, I lost track of the time. What is happening to me?

My Stats:

2 volunteers who solved a mystery

1 notebook for writing down stuff I don't completely understand

0 balloons above Neda's desk

1 camera with lots of buttons

1 photography class I might take

1 kind of cool community project that still might be temporary

Mood: Baffled that I forgot about the Spirit Week meeting and guilty that I abandoned Ella.

13

Snollygoster

As I hustle to science, I am still feeling awful about missing the Spirit Week meeting. Ella promises me that not that much happened at the meeting, but it sure sounded like a lot. They decided on a theme for the dance, along with colors, and made up some kind of seventh-grade cheer.

My backpack is extra heavy because I have Dad's camera in there. Auggie, Graeme, and Justin are a little ways ahead of me in the crowded hall. When I squint my eyes, their shoes blur together. I wonder if there's a way to capture that with the camera.

Milton P. shuffles toward me, various airliner tags on his backpack flapping up and down. As he's about to pass the boys, he clutches his shoe box tightly.

Auggie smiles at Milton P., now only an arm's length away by the trophy case. I hate how cute Auggie looks when he smiles. I do not want to think Auggie is cute.

"Snollygoster," he asks Milton P. in a light, happy voice, "bring an extra pair of Nikes for me?"

"Yeah, dude," Justin says. "But I need a larger size. Do you have it in a ten?"

"No!" Face reddening, Milton P. freezes in front of Auggie. "There are no shoes in here. I have told you that for the one thousandth time!"

I start to speed up when I remember I have a test in science. Did I leave my prep sheet back in my locker? We're allowed one page of notes when we take the test.

I sit down on the bench and unzip my backpack to see if my prep sheet is inside, and I hear Graeme say, "What's in the box, Snollygoster? Something top secret? Keeping it from the government?"

I try to focus, pawing through my backpack and pulling out my big binder. Please. Please let my notes for the test be in there.

"Tell us, Snollygoster," says Justin.

Milton P. squeezes his cauliflower-white hands. "Never."

Seven minutes to get to science class. Whew. Okay. I did put my notes for the test into my binder.

I stand to go when Graeme dashes up to Milton P. and grabs his arm. I freeze in place. "Hang on, buddy," he says in a syrupy voice. "We just want to talk."

"Yeah, your shirt coordinates nicely with your shoe box." Justin smiles. Graeme doesn't let go of his hold on Milton, who's red-faced and desperately trying to pull away. I frown at what I'm hearing.

"Let go of me. Get off!" Milton P. cries.

I open my mouth but hesitate.

Auggie whispers something to Justin and Graeme. They're shaking their heads and laughing. My stomach burns with anger. Okay, I've had enough of them. Really.

I cross my arms. "What are you guys doing?"

Auggie looks at Graeme, who looks at Justin. "Just being friendly," says Auggie, shrugging as a few kids thread around them.

Milton shakes out of Graeme's grasp, then backs away and continues down the hall.

That's when Justin sticks out his red basketball shoe.

Milton tumbles to the floor. His hands smack the

tiles. I gasp along with kids passing by who slow down or stop walking altogether to stare.

He rolls like a log. The shoe box catapults out of his hands, skids across the floor five feet in front of him, and spins upside down. Somehow the lid stays on. A water bottle rolls toward the trophy case. I race over to Milton P.

From the other kids I hear, "That must have hurt" and "Ow."

I crouch next to Milton P. My backpack slumps to the floor. His eyes are closed. I wish I knew CPR because he's not moving. Auggie and his buddies shove forward to look.

I shake his arm gently. "Are you okay?"

"Sorry," says Auggie. He's come up behind us.

Milton P.'s eyes open and his apple-red cheeks turn even redder. Breathing hard, he sits up. He blinks. "I am fine," he barks. But his eyes glisten.

I glare at Auggie and Justin and Graeme. Now that Milton P. is sitting up and seems okay enough, people continue on their way to the next class.

"You all right?" I ask Milton P. again.

He peers at me in a way I don't understand. Milton P. scrambles for his shoe box, but some kid in a baseball cap strolling past accidentally stumbles over it. The box skids farther from him.

"Sorry," the kid mutters, and continues down the hall.

Milton P. curls his hands into fists.

"Dude, I'm so sorry," says Auggie. He sprints over to the shoe box and grabs it. He jogs over to hand it to Milton P., but Justin swipes it from Auggie.

"Looky looky what I got." Justin shakes the box.

Milton P. scrambles down the hall. He grabs at the shoe box.

But Justin clutches it over his head. "What could be inside?" He juggles the box.

"Stop it!" I stand and yell as Milton P. claws at Justin, who lifts it higher over his head. "Money, candy, or Pokémon cards?" muses Justin.

The warning bell rings. Five more minutes to get to class.

Justin begins to lift a corner of the lid. My heart thuds in my chest. Auggie and Graeme look at each other with surprised expressions.

"NOOOOOOO!" screams Milton P. so loudly that I think the trophy case in the hallway has begun to shake. Justin holds the box out in front of him as if it's a bomb that might explode.

One of the secretaries, Mrs. Ozer, rushes out of the office. Justin drops the box. Something rattles inside.

Milton P. screams again.

"What's going on?" Mrs. Ozer's eyebrows furrow as she sweeps her graying, hippie-long hair off her shoulder.

"It's okay," says Auggie, nodding at Justin. "He didn't look. The lid's still on."

She glares at Justin. "Give that back to Milton P. right now." Everyone knows about Milton P.'s shoe box.

Justin grabs the box and pushes it at Milton P. Then he backs up with his hands raised. "I was just messing around."

"Are you okay, dear?" Mrs. Ozer asks Milton P.

His eyes dart around everywhere as if looking for an escape. "Yeah." Milton P. checks inside the box to see if the contents are okay. His glasses steam up so that his eyes appear as blurry bits of blue. There are only three minutes until class now.

"Justin grabbed it away from him," I say, fuming, my heart pounding. "He tripped him."

"It was an accident," protests Justin.

Mrs. Ozer glares at Justin. "If I hear another word from you boys, I'm going to bring you in for a little chat with Principal Wallace."

"We're sorry," gushes Auggie. "Really."

Milton P. continues to stare at the contents of the box. His face twists as if whatever is inside may be dying. He looks as if he wants to bolt, but probably the secretary standing there makes him stay in his spot.

I glance nervously up at the clock. I've got to get to class.

"Sorry, Milton P." Justin smiles sheepishly. "We were just playing."

"We're supersorry," adds Auggie. Staring at his feet, Graeme nods.

"Okay, get to third period," says Mrs. Ozer as she makes a shooing motion. She glances around at the few kids still left hurrying to class. To everyone she announces, "You've got three minutes until the last bell." Then she scurries back inside the office.

Milton P. picks up his backpack. Beads of sweat dot his forehead. Auggie grabs the water bottle that skidded out of Milton P.'s lunch bag. Wow. Maybe Auggie feels badly about what happened.

Milton P. stares down Auggie. "Do. Not. Help. Me!" His eyes fix on the water bottle that Auggie holds out to him. "Put it down."

Auggie sets the water bottle on the ground. Scooping

it up, Milton P. plods away down the hall. I want to cheer for Milton P.

"Wow, Justin," Auggie says. Only he doesn't say *wow*. He says a word much worse than *wow*. "Why did you do that?" he whispers, and glances at the door to the office. Justin fidgets. "You shouldn't have tried to look in his box, dude," says Auggie.

Justin throws up his hands. "You told me to trip him." Folding his arms over his chest, he harrumphs.

"Is that true?" I stare down the hall where Milton P. disappeared and think about catching up with him. But first I whirl around and face Auggie. "You guys are such jerks. I can't believe you'd be so mean."

"It was a joke. Seriously. I didn't think he'd"— Auggie glances at Justin—"actually do it."

Of course he would. He'll do anything Auggie says. He's just a follower. I look up at a clock in the hall. The final bell to end break is about to ring. I seriously have one minute to get to class.

I race around the corner to try to catch up with Milton P. I call out to him. He went in the opposite direction of where I need to go. I could just zip to class and barely make it on time. Or go see if Milton P. is okay.

I decide to go after Milton P., but he's long gone.

Only a few stragglers hurry past in the hallway now. The bell rings and I feel three things at once. First, I feel terror at getting a tardy on a test day. Second, I feel bad for Milton P. because tears, actual tears, had been sliding down his apple-red cheeks under his fogged-up glasses.

And third, I'm curious because I'm dying—*dying*—to know what is actually in that shoe box.

Lunch Strategy Session

We're sitting at the table next to the Quick Cart discussing Spirit Week with Bailey and the Bees. Nobody is saying anything about me missing the meeting at Bailey's house. But honestly, I'm still feeling superbad about it. Then Megan asks if I'm going to have to miss more meetings, and I tell her definitely not, but I'm not sure she believes me.

Megan waves a pretzel stick. She's smiling at everyone, including Ella. But she never makes eye contact with me. "You guys, I've gotten even more volunteers to help set up and decorate before the dance."

"I'm getting lots of parents to bring snacks and drinks," says Janel. "I'll make a store run with Mrs.

Grayson for ice and paper goods on Wednesday before the dance. And we'll pick up the hot dogs for the contest then too."

"Perfect," says Bailey. She stirs her yogurt and shakes her head. Some of her hair has escaped her ponytail and forms a glistening halo. I'd love to whip out my dad's camera and take a photo of it, but I'd feel too embarrassed.

"Did you see the canned food pyramids by the front office?" asks Bailey.

"Oh yeah," says Megan. "The eighth grade one is scary big."

Ella's shoulders slump. My shoulders slump. "Don't worry." I dip my carrots in some hummus. "I have a plan. Ella and I—"

"You mean tracking your old followers and telling them to mail in cans?" snaps Ella. She is obviously mad about something.

"Well, I was mostly joking about that," I say. "But listen to this idea. I thought it'd be better and more dramatic if the seventh grade brought our cans all at once, so the eighth grade can't see it coming."

"I get you," says Janel. "Like a surprise attack of cans."

"Exactly." I take another bite of my carrot.

"What day?" Bailey sips her water.

"The last day to bring in cans is Wednesday, March twenty-first," I say. "That's twelve days from now, right in the middle of Spirit Week. So I think we should bring in a massive amount of cans on Wednesday morning and spread the word. The Great Canned Food Sneak Attack."

Bailey claps. "I'm loving it, people. It's supersneaky!"

"And!" I say, raising my hand like we're in class. "Maybe you could do a survey. Like, what does Spirit Week mean to you? And then we could get quotes from people and have them read at the Spirit Rally." Suddenly I think about taking photos of the kids.

Bailey squints her eyes. "Sounds good. The bell's about to ring."

And then I realize something. I really do want to take that photography class. Because if I took that class, I'd probably take the best photos ever, even better than I do now. I'm going to sign up after school.

I text in my mind: *Don't let anything stop you!* Maybe that's what Moses was thinking out there in the desert.

My Stats:

111 followers on seventh-grade Spirit Week page

800ish followers on eighth-grade Spirit Week page—I can't bear to look to see if it's gone up more

233 LIKES on Auggie's canned food shot

1 mystery of what was in the shoe box

1 camera in my backpack that I'm dying to use

1 photography class I'm going to sign up for!

Mood: Scared about the seventh grade's chances, but excited about my photography class!

14

Open Your Eyes

I'm ten minutes early for the photography class and almost all of the seats are already filled. The instructor is a tall, skinny dude with a long blond ponytail and a tiny bit of hair on his chin that looks like a fuzzy caterpillar. I think it's called a soul patch. But I don't know why. It doesn't seem that soulful to me. The teacher stands in front, tapping on the podium as if it's a drum. He looks as though he should be teaching a class on rock and roll.

Everyone has their notebook and pencils out on their desks. Whoops, I forgot to bring a notebook. Everyone looks a little older than me, except for a girl with one long braid. She looks my age, and a kid fiddling with a huge telephoto lens looks like he knows things. He's probably our age too. I scoot past him and can feel his eyes on me. Probably wondering about the portfolio that I'm clutching. I sit down in one of the few vacant desks toward the back. My camera, slung around my shoulder, rests on my lap, and I put my portfolio on the desk. Last night I had spent an hour putting it together, choosing the best photos. Most of my photos that I took with Floyd are gone, but I do have some on my photostream on the family computer.

I glance up at the clock above the whiteboard. There are still seven minutes before class starts. I have time to ask the teacher what he thinks of my work.

Maybe I should wait until after class, when everyone is gone.

No, I can't let Mom wait in the car like that.

I steal another glance at the instructor. He's a real photographer. Right here, now, standing in front of me. This proves my uncle Eric, the very successful dentist who lives in Florida, is wrong. You can make a living taking pictures. This guy proves it.

It's now or never. *Go for it*, a little voice in my head cries. I sidle around the desks, then whiz up to my teacher. "I wanted to show you my photos," I say all in a rush, my heart beating fast.

The real, live-in-person photographer peers down at me. I'm tall for my age, but this guy is taller. Up close I see his hair isn't blond at all, but white and gray. He's actually kind of old-looking, but in an aging rock star way.

My arms get jittery and my throat goes dry. "I want to know what you think of my work. Whether you like it."

"Put it away," he says in a clipped British accent. His eyes skim my portfolio.

"But—"

"You'll understand in a minute." He glances up at the clock.

My heart sinks. I thought that was the point of being here. I don't get it. Burrowing into my hoodie, I slink back to my seat.

Only someone else is sitting in it, a stocky guy with one earring in his left ear. "That's my desk," I say, my voice coming out high and whiny like a little kid. "I sat here first." The stocky guy looks at me blankly as if I'm not fully formed. "Didn't see your stuff," he says after a long pause.

And then he doesn't move. My desk. My chair. I got here earlier than him.

A girl in the front row with streaks of purple in her hair whips around. She wears lots of black rubberlike rings around her arms. "There's a space next to me."

"Thanks," I say. But I'm not feeling so happy about it. The seat is right in front of the teacher who does not want to see my photos.

I take in a huge breath. I blink extra hard so I will not cry. This class is not off to a good start for me. I sit down in my new seat and fiddle around with my camera. Behind me, I can hear the desk-stealer saying, "Hey you, with the pink hoodie. Don't I know you?"

Okay, I'm wearing a pink hoodie. He's definitely speaking to me, but I decide to ignore him.

A round-faced girl on my other side fans herself with a magazine. "It's like a sauna in here."

"Too warm," says someone else from the back row.

The teacher who does not want to look at my photos says, "You have two choices. Either too hot or too cold. Like life." Some kids laugh. I don't. "So." He points to the whiteboard. "My name is Ren Litman and this is going to be a dedicated month of photography. It's going to be quite a bit of fun and we're going to cover miles of ground."

Yeah, and stomp all over me while doing it.

"But I want to make something clear." He glances in my direction. "I will not tell you if I like your photos, or whether I detest your photos, or whether I think they're extremely mediocre. Essentially, it doesn't matter whether I like something or not. It only matters whether you like it. Not me. Not the mail carrier. Not your mother. Or your friends."

My face flushes. Yes. He is talking right to me. Ugh.

"However, if you ask me a question about the depth of field or different framing options or proportions, I'll tell you more than you'll want to hear. But I will not give you my opinion on the quality of your work."

There are murmurs of surprise and my cheeks grow warm. He's definitely saying this because of me. "You will see why I feel strongly about this in a moment," says Ren. "But first, I want you to write down five activities you enjoy doing."

Pencil and pens scratch on paper.

Well, I know what I don't enjoy doing. Right now I'm not enjoying being in this class. The pens and pencils continue to scrawl on notepads. But I'm not going to do this. This is dumb. This has nothing—*nothing*—to do with photography. I fold my arms in front of me so he'll see how dumb this question is. Suddenly I'm happy, thrilled that I forgot my little spiral notebook.

"And the second thing I want you to write about is your background in photography. What you have done, and what you'd like to know."

Well, the thousands of comments and LIKES on my photos on Snappypic are gone. In a black hole somewhere. That's what I know. My skin prickles so much it hurts.

"So we're going to keep it simple." He steeples his fingers and pauses dramatically. "I've got three basic rules of photography. The first rule." He pauses again. "If you take a photo and you like it, it's a good photo. That's it. A fun memory at the seashore? Brilliant!" He rolls the pen in his hand and taps the whiteboard. "Next rule. Oh, I hate the word *rule*. Next *concept* I'm going to tell you. You don't need to wait for a special occasion to take a photo. Tap into your interests and bring your camera to it. If you have a thing for monster trucks, start shooting away at them. If you like cookies and candy bars, then start taking pictures of that."

He pauses again, almost daring us to speak. Nobody does. Nobody.

I think about taking pictures of cookies. Would I like that? Maybe. I do like cookies, especially white chocolate chip with macadamia nuts.

"This isn't going to be a class where I'm going to bring in a vase and a bunch of oranges and apples and you're going to snap away. You're going to practice on your own. You're going to go out there and find out what makes you sing, at a cellular level."

I thought we were going to be learning stuff like the best kind of zoom to buy, not a talk on making my cells sing. That's crazy-talk. And yet cool.

Someone's hand shoots up. "What if you don't know what you like?"

"Then figure it out." Suddenly there is something so familiar about the teacher. And then I remember why. He's the photographer from Milton P.'s bar mitzvah.

Ren strolls between the aisles. "This is the best time in the history of photography to be taking pictures. Period. The *very* best time. Does anybody know why?"

Once again his eyes dare us to speak. But I know, and so does everybody else, that we are not supposed to. I gaze up at a poster on the wall of a guy snowboarding. It says: SUCCESS IS GETTING UP JUST ONE MORE TIME THAN YOU FALL DOWN. Somehow it's a funny thought, because

I'm picturing a bunch of photographers falling down, cracking their lenses.

But I try not to laugh because Ren has a very serious look on his face.

He taps his chin. "I'm going to show you why this is the best time in the history of photography to take pictures. Look. And listen."

He points his camera to the ceiling. And *click. Click. Click. Click. Click. Click. Click. Click. Click. Click.* It continues clicking about a bazillion times. Ren shoots and shoots and shoots. Maybe a hundred shots right there of the ceiling.

Finally he stops and puts the camera on the podium. A huge smile stretches across his face. "To develop what I just shot? It'd cost a massive amount of money. So go out and practice as much as you like. What is it going to cost you? A new memory card?"

I'm suddenly feeling lucky.

Ren clasps his hands together. "You don't need to wait for a special photo trip. You'll start appreciating all the little things around you. You can really enjoy what has become familiar to you. Your camera can shoot whether your eyes are open or closed. It's your choice."

Then he lets out a big breath and has us get into

small groups where we are supposed to talk about what we want to take photos of and our previous experience in photography. I tell the girls in my group that I like taking photos of things that make other people happy. I mentally picture all of the comments that I got when I took a photo of the baby bunny I found in the yard. It was crazy. Everyone loved it. The girl who was too hot says she likes taking candid photos of people when they're singing or talking, and the girl with the purple hair says she loves nests of all kinds.

Then I say, "I bet Ren doesn't do Snappypic. He doesn't seem to care about LIKES."

"I doubt that," says the girl with purple streaks. "But I think what he means is you want others to enjoy you for you, right? So if I'm into elephants and somebody else is too, then they really might like my elephant photos."

I nod. I think I get what she means.

The desk-stealer in the back suddenly points at me and says in a loud voice, "I swear I know you."

"Sorry." I shake my head.

Photo Lens Boy says, "Yeah, she does look familiar."

"The guys in this class are weird," I whisper to my group. "I've never seen any of them before in my life."

My desk partners give me these looks, like maybe they don't believe me. When we're done, the purple-haired girl asks Ren what we should do next.

"Whatever you want," he says. "You can leave. You can chitchat. You may ask me questions."

I glance at the clock. It's supposed to go another fifteen minutes.

"It isn't time to go," says the too-warm girl.

"Well, aren't you fortunate?" Ren grins. "You get to be rid of me sooner tonight. Because that's all I have to tell you now. Next class, I'm going to go over the history of photography. So go forth and take photos."

Okay, it's weird. My heart is beating extra fast and I'm excited. I'm excited about going forth and discovering what kinds of pictures I really want to take.

My Stats:
0 notebooks
1 photography teacher who won't tell me what he thinks of my photos
5 things I'm supposed to like but don't know yet
5 weeks in a class that's weird and very cool all at the same time

1 camera that I'm itching to take photos with all weekend!

Mood: Kind of excited to find out what makes my cells sing and to make sure they don't sing totally off-key.

15

More Milton P.

Over the weekend, I was a photo-taking machine. I strolled around our yard shooting close-ups of bark. The rose trellis. The lid of the recycling bin. Over Saturday and Sunday, I must have taken hundreds of photos.

Some of them weren't great. Well, actually, most of them weren't. I couldn't get anything in full sun to come out right, but the ones in the shade of a tree or when the clouds rolled in worked better. I fooled around with using flash and not using flash.

I printed out probably a dozen of my best and put the photos in an accordion file. I'm really proud of them.

During school, I'm also in full photo mode. On Monday between classes, I took a ton of pictures, even during lunch.

After third period on Tuesday, I snap a bunch of shots in the hall and lose track of time, so I hurry to Bailey's table. Now I'll only have fifteen minutes to eat my lunch.

I slide into my seat next to Ella and let out a breath. Famished, I pull food out of my lunch bag.

"Where were you?" asks Ella.

"Oh, just taking photos," I say. "You know, for my class."

"Well, I got worried." Ella wipes her mouth with a napkin. "You didn't let anyone know."

"Sorry." I shrug.

"Spirit Week is coming right up," says Bailey.

"I know," I say.

"Ella's posting a schedule," Janel says, crunching a carrot.

"Oh, that's great," I murmur. "I didn't know about that."

Bailey glances at her notebook. "We've got to make our final push. I hear that the eighth-grade chair is making a giant banner. It's going to say something like 'Eighth Grade Rocks Spirit Week!'"

Megan leans into the group. "You guys, does anyone know what the sixth graders are up to? I've hardly heard anything. Should we be worried?"

I absently play with my straw "I so wouldn't worry. Yesterday I saw that girl with pigtails. Gina. She was having a meeting. Want to know what they were doing?"

Bailey fiddles with her scarf. "What? Tell us."

"They were having a handstand contest." I shake my head.

Bailey rolls her eyes. "You've got to be kidding."

"Auggie and his friends are all going to play ukulele on Crazy Hair Day to get everyone into Spirit Week," says Megan. I laugh at the idea as I tear into my turkey wrap.

"Graeme and Justin know how to play?" asks Janel.

Megan giggles. "No, but that never stops them."

Bailey consults her notebook and shakes her head. "One week to get ready. I've still got to get my stuff for Crazy Hair Day."

"It's going to be *so* much fun," says Megan. Kids at the next table hide their phones as Mr. Chase patrols around the circular tables with his walkie-talkie squawking.

"I'm going to put wires in my hair so my braids stick right up," says Janel.

"I'm going for rainbow hair," says Megan.

"I have this purple wig that's really outrageous," says Ella. Her voice is definitely less tentative as she talks about her Crazy Hair ideas.

"How about you, Karma?" asks Megan, who munches on some caramel corn.

"Oh, it's going to be a surprise. I plan to out-crazy everyone." Of course, I've been so busy I have no idea what that will be, but I'll figure it out.

A Muddy Life

I'm with Dorina up in the stacks of the historical society. She's showing me how to search through the historical research index (HRI). I biked over right after school. Anna is working downstairs with a bunch of volunteers getting ready for a rummage sale over the weekend. They're selling donated items they don't need. Since I brought my camera with me, I snapped shots of everyone setting up the sale items like old hats, typewriters, and stacks of books. I got great candids, including one of Karen in her banana earrings modeling a boa and a volunteer with a bushy mustache in a top hat.

Dorina motions me over from where I'm standing to the corner of the room. Her feather earrings swing back and forth as she flips through a giant binder plunked in the center of a small table. "So now I'll show you what's in the PFs."

"PFs?" I ask. "What's that?"

"The photo files." Dorina points to a row of cabinets along the left wall. They are the same shade of gray as her sweater-vest.

The photo files. Cool. That's what I've been waiting for this whole time

I start to sit down at a table when Neda appears. Today she's wearing a navy blazer and matching skirt. She looks even more official than normal. Her lipstick is as orange as ever.

"I understand you take very good notes," she says. Through her black frames, she's peering at my pad of paper. Her eyes look big and extra owly.

"Um. Yes. Thanks," I say.

Neda adjusts a giant accordion file she's holding. "I'm glad you're getting an overview of the photos since I have something in mind for you later."

I nod. I'm surprised that Neda has anything in mind for me other than leaving her precious historical society.

Maybe that's it. She's going to show me the door and wave bye-bye.

"So have at it!" Neda says, then clicks down downstairs in her high heels.

"Do you know what she wants me to do later?" I ask Dorina.

"I don't know." She shrugs. "Okay, then." Dorina points to a filing cabinet behind me. "Here's where we keep the PFs." She pulls out a blue binder. "This is the index." She hands it to me. I flip through. Inside there's a listing of all the contents. "You need gloves for the ephemera boxes too," I say, remembering what Dorina said last time.

"Exactly." She pats my shoulder. "You got it!"

I like "getting" things. I walk over to a table. A box of vinyl exam gloves sits on it as if we're at a hospital. I grab a pair and plop them down on the tabletop. Pulling out my camera, I adjust the focal length and take a close-up of the gloves. It's a sharp, frame-filling shot. The texture of the rubber looks so cool. And from the light of a nearby lamp, they almost gleam. As Dorina searches for something in the stacks, I take a quick candid, focusing on her profile. I tuck my camera back in my bag before Dorina turns around to face me.

She taps her hand on a shelf filled with fat books. "We have quite a few photographic tomes."

"Can I look?"

"Of course." Dorina pulls out a couple of volumes and I stride over to her.

After Dorina sets the heavy books down on a nearby table, I flip through them. It looks like the area right outside of Portland. One is a shot of what's probably the Hood River, because a snow-capped Mount Hood towers in the background. Dorina stands over my shoulder, looking down at the rest of the images with me.

"I recognize that bridge," I say excitedly. "It's that one near the park downtown. Only instead of cars going over it, there are buggies." And horses. In another photo there's a steam engine. "The street isn't exactly a street. It looks sort of—"

"Muddy." Dorina turns the page to another street scene. "Definitely no pavement back then."

"Everything must have gotten so messy."

"Oh my, yes. The mud wrestled its way down the streets in the winter, I can tell you that much."

I imagine a bunch of people in old-fashioned Western clothes covered in dirt. "My little brother would have loved it. We call him Pigpen."

Dorina laughs. "So would my little granddaughter. She can't leave mud alone."

I try to imagine living back then. "It's weird, but for some reason I think of the past in black and white."

"That's because of photos." Dorina flips through more pages. "But if you go farther back before photography, all of our documents are paintings or sketches. So if you think of those wonderful Renaissance paintings by Da Vinci, then I bet you think of the past as looking like a colorful oil painting."

"You're so right!"

I spend the rest of the time flipping through the old photos in the PFs. I'm starting to see a pattern. There are images of families. And of railroads. Of farms. Street scenes. Businesses. Schools.

"So . . . having fun?" asks a voice.

I turn around. It's Neda. She has the ability to pop out of nowhere. You'd think I'd hear her in those heels.

Neda takes off her glasses and twirls them. "Ready for your project?"

The mystery project? "Sure," I say.

"You get to dig into some more photos." Neda points to the other side of Anna's desk. "Everyone dumps their stuff here. Someone dies and they figure we want everything. We don't. Last year we got four pianos and a book on Wyoming history." She shakes her head and her hair stays perfectly in place. "Oh, and we got four broken mops."

"I guess they thought the mops were historic?"

She laughs. "Yes, we just usually put up a sign and sell what we can't use. Or give it away."

She points to a couple of cardboard boxes that are completely full. "We have no idea what's in there. We just know they are photos. They were just dropped off yesterday. So are you up for some sorting?"

"Sure," I say again, even though I'm feeling a little unsure.

"The key thing is we want to keep only what is related to county history."

Yikes! "I don't know if I can do this," I protest. "How am I going to know if it's county history?"

"Ah, that's why this job is a good one for you. You're going to be the first sorter. So one of the things I'm going to want you to do is take out photos that obviously are not county history and put them into a pile. So, for example, if you see someone standing under a palm tree on a sandy white beach . . ."

"Set it aside," I say.

"Or if they're standing next to the Statue of Liberty."

"Set it aside."

Neda smiles. "You got it."

"What does the historical society do with the stuff you don't need?"

"Well, Anna belongs to some LISTSERVs and lets other organizations know what we have. And if a museum or historical society wants something, we'll send them out."

"So it's like a big historical online social network."

"Exactly. So in addition to the obviously not-from-around-here pile, you're going to make other ones too. You'll have a pile for family portraits. Farms. Businesses. Landscapes. Basically, you're going to spread everything out on this table." She points to a large table on the other side of Anna's desk. "And if you see something interesting, put it in a separate pile."

"So I do all of this? By myself?"

Neda folds her arms and nods. "Yes. You."

Suddenly I feel sort of important, like I'm deciding history. I'm deciding what gets remembered, what stays and what goes, and suddenly it feels like a big responsibility, but maybe one I can handle.

I start sorting the photos. The street scenes are easy,

but the family portraits are slower going. Not because it's hard to figure out, but because I like studying them. In one there's a girl my age with a big bonnet and a mysterious smile. She looks like someone I'd want to be friends with. Plus, she has a little brother with flipped-up hair and a smudge on his face, like he tried to get his hair to stay down but couldn't. He reminds me of Toby. These are the ultimate Throwback Thursday pics.

Dorina puts on a pair of gloves and inspects my piles. "You like those, don't you."

"Yes," I say. "I really do. I even signed up for that photography class!"

She tilts her head and her feather earrings swing. "You did? Why, that's wonderful, sweetie."

Someone hurries up the stairs. It's Neda. She clicks up to us in her high heels. "What's wonderful?"

Dorina neatens a stack of photos. "Oh, Karma signed up for a photography class."

"Aha, that's why she was photographing everyone downstairs getting ready for the rummage sale."

I feel my ears warm. "Yes," I admit.

Neda folds her arms in front of her neatly pressed suit. She peers up at the clock. "It's almost five. I can't believe how fast time flies around here." Pivoting to face me, she smiles. Actually smiles. No trout pucker. "So, Karma, how was your first official day?"

"Good." Then I stand up. "Wait? Did you say official?"

Neda clasps her hands together and makes a steeple with her fingers. "Normally, as I mentioned, we don't like to take in very young students. But when they are mature, we're happy to make an exception."

Then she clicks away.

I turn to Dorina. "I think I'm in."

"Of course you are, dear." She pats my shoulder. "Of course you are."

My Stats:

4 mops left at the historical society

Gazillions of old photos

1 pair of gloves worn to look at the photos

1 volunteer named Dorina who loves purple

1 girl who's a little nervous about all of this responsibility

Mood: Mostly superhappy that I'm now an official person

16

Overwhelmed

I suddenly feel a little guilty. All week I've been spending so much time at the historical society and reading books on cameras and learning about my camera and taking photos that I don't have too much time to think about Spirit Week stuff, like the seventh-grade Snappypic page. During lunch today and yesterday, I spent time in the library getting more photography books.

Ella and the Bees have been giving me worried looks.

But I can tell most kids are getting excited about Spirit Week. The different grade committees are plastering the school with posters. Kids are jabbering away about who they are going to be twins with on Twin Day and how crazy they're going to make their hair on Crazy Hair Day.

What's really crazy is that I'm looking forward to working at the historical society again next week. Also, Dorina asked me if I wanted to help work at the annual rummage sale this weekend. She's expecting a ton of people to show up since the newspaper listed it in their events section. I said yes immediately. Even crazier? I haven't really thought about Floyd.

Milton P. Approaches

I'm over at the taco bar, reaching for the shredded cheese. Lunch started about ten minutes ago, and over at our table, Bailey, Megan, Ella, and Janel huddle together, laughing hysterically about a joke that I don't get. It's one of those you-had-to-be-there moments.

And the problem was, I wasn't there. Yesterday after volunteering at the historical society, I forgot to go to the meeting at Bailey's house. Again. It definitely looks bad. I just got caught up in what I was doing.

I feel terrible about it, but at least Ella posted the

whole Spirit Week schedule to all of the seventh-grade followers and designed some new Crazy Hair posters, which she has since put up.

Mr. Chase's walkie-talkie crackles as he parades around the perimeter of the lunchroom.

As I edge around the taco bar, Milton P. trudges up to me with his shoe box. His glasses are smudged, but that doesn't stop him from locking eyes with me. He points over to his table, where Owen Matthews is chewing with his mouth open. "You can sit with us."

"Oh." I reposition my backpack. "Uh, thanks. I'm sitting over there." I point to the Quick Cart. "I was just doing . . . something else." I pat my camera bag.

Milton P.'s lips pull into a real smile. "Too bad. We could have talked about what to do with irregular pieces and parts."

"Parts?" I drop my backpack carefully on the ground.

"I've got lots of LEGO pieces that are one of a kind," says Milton P. Kids weave around us as they head toward the double doors.

"Oh, LEGOs." Toby would actually love to talk to Milton P. Dad always helps Toby with his complicated LEGO sets. Now that Milton P.'s dad is gone, I wonder who helps him. I get a hollow feeling thinking about it. But really, Milton P. probably doesn't need help with LEGOs anymore. From across the cafeteria, Ella glances over at me. Her eyebrows arch as if she's trying to figure something out. She's probably thinking, *Karma disappeared for most of lunch taking photos, only to spend her time talking to Milton P.?*

"Okay, good-bye," says Milton P. "You can sit with us. Any time. It is a very nice table."

"Got it." I hike my bags back onto my shoulders and trudge to our table. But as I do, Bailey and the Bees get up to leave and wander over to another table. Ella is still sitting down. "Where did they all go?" I ask.

"They're reminding people about Spirit Week," Ella explains.

I swallow hard. That should have been my job.

"Karma, lunch is almost over," Ella says. "What happened to you?"

"I was taking photos. You know, for my class." I slump into my seat and pull my sandwich out of my bag.

"Must have been lots of them." Ella glances up at the clock on the opposite wall. "You better eat. The bell's going to ring soon."

"Ow." I tap my shoulder blades. "My back hurts."

"Probably from carrying too many books in your backpack," says Ella.

"They're on photography. I need them right now. So how's the seventh-grade Snappypic going?"

"Pretty good. I started posting a ton. I just reminded people that Crazy Hair Day is on Monday."

"Sorry," I say. "That was my job. I've just been so busy."

"It's okay," says Ella. "I got it done."

As Bailey and the Bees sit back down at our table, they are deep in conversation. "Some people are just flakes," Bailey is saying. Are they talking about me? The girls immediately stop talking when they see me. The back of my neck heats up.

Janel balls up her napkin. "I heard Auggie's posting a ukulele song on YouTube this afternoon," says Janel. "It's an eighth-grade Spirit Week song."

"It'll probably be silly." I wipe my mouth with my napkin.

"But funny." Megan frowns as she pushes bread-crumbs into a tiny pile on her tray.

"Megan and I started a Crazy Hair Day video. Karma, could you post that?" Janel asks.

"Maybe," I say, "but I'm not so sure I can get onto Snappypic this weekend."

Bailey glances at her Spirit Week clipboard. "On Monday, Karma, could you at least take pictures of everyone's crazy hair?"

"Sure," I say, thumping my camera case. "Now that's something I can definitely do."

> Posting

I stand by the front office waiting for Mom to pick me up for my orthodontist appointment. With my camera, I'm focusing in on the seventh-grade tower of cans. Okay, it's more like a stack. *Click. Click.* I snap a couple of shots. Mom should be here any second. Putting down my camera, I can't help staring at the giant tower of cans that the eighth grade collected.

Okay, relax, Karma.

Seriously. Let it go.

My Stats:

1 more Spirit Week meeting missed

5 weird looks that Ella gave me

1 small stack of seventh-grade cans

QUEEN OF LIKES

1 medium stack of sixth-grade cans
1 giant tower of eighth-grade cans
1 backpack full of books and my camera

Mood: Can't wait until Monday. Spirit Week! Or am
I kind of losing interest???

17

The History of Seeing

This time I get to my photography class fifteen minutes early and do not leave my seat. Already it's been a photography sort of day. This morning I went to the historical society and helped out with the rummage sale. It was drizzling but the sun peeked out, so it was a warm rain. A dozen volunteers laid everything for the sale under blue tents in the parking lot. My family came by for a bit but I was too busy to really chat with them. My job was to ask potential customers if they needed help finding anything, but mostly I snapped photos. I ended up shooting more than a hundred images of things and people. To compose the pictures, I moved around, trying different positions and camera angles. I got some really fun candids of Dorina and Karen, the other volunteers, and even a few customers. I even got one of Neda smiling broadly as she sold a stack of musty and ripped-up books. It's amazing how much people will pay for old stuff.

Waiting for Ren to start, I glance around, making sure that the desk-stealer is not eyeing my chair. I'm sitting next to the purple-haired girl in the front row again. Nothing embarrassing will happen to me this time.

Ren hops up from behind his desk. Today he's wearing cowboy boots and they thump on the floor as he shuffles to the podium. I guess he thinks he's a British cowboy.

Everyone in the class gets quiet.

"Today, as promised," he says in his clipped accent, "we'll be discussing the history of photography." I give the purple-haired girl a look. Her name is Veena. The whole time? History? I get a lot of that at the historical society.

Ren pulls down a screen that whizzes over the whiteboard.

"Can't we get to the taking photos part?" I whisper,

and Veena nods. What is it with history? Why is every-one obsessed with the past? Back then everyone made mistakes.

Behind me, the desk-stealer calls out, "Hey, you in the pink hoodie. I know you."

Heads turn to stare at me.

"Yeah, I know her too," says Photo Lens Boy.

Ren's voice cuts in. "Save the chitchat for later."

I feel the tips of my ears redden. Not sure what they are thinking but these boys definitely don't know me. What's their problem?

"Okay, then. Let's begin." Ren grips the podium as if he's afraid it's about to topple over any second. "Some people think that photography started in the 1800s." He leans forward, checking to see if we are those sort of people.

Um, not me. To be honest, I never really thought about it. Seems like cameras have always been around, like bread or milk or orange juice.

"Any guesses on when photography actually started?" He drums his fingers. Ren explains how it started in fifth-century China and something about refracting light. I'm not sure I'm totally following. He also explains that a camera is just a box with a little hole.

Some people laugh at that.

Then he moves onto the Renaissance and perspective and talks about how everything used to look before that, in terms of paintings.

Whoa. There was a time, long ago, when everything looked flat? This is blowing my mind.

Then he goes on about a camera obscura and wet plates and daguerreotypes. Suddenly I'm feeling like I'm in high school, or even college. Some old photos flash up on the screen. They look like the black-and-white ones at the historical society. The girls wear lace-up boots. The high-collared dresses look like curtains with tassels.

"The world is different because of photography." Ren claps his hand so loudly that anyone asleep is now definitely awake. "Why?"

"Before you had to paint a scene or a person if you wanted to remember it or fix it in time," says Veena.

"It's a way to share stuff," says a boy in the back row. Everyone has an opinion.

"It's a way to express yourself."

"Politicians use images for their campaigns."

"And companies use it to get you to buy their stuff."

Ren smiles. "Yes, all of that."

Next he tells us to get into small groups and talk about how photography has changed us.

I'm in the group with Erin and Veena. Erin talks more about rotten skinny model photos, and Veena says that she loves photos that take her someplace she's never been. I'm about to say what I think when Photo Lens Boy yells out, "Hey, Pink Hoodie, I know where I know you from."

I whip around to tell him to shut up.

Photo Lens Boy points at me. "You're that girl at Merton on Snappypic all the time."

"You had a gazillion followers," adds the desk-stealer.

My heart is pounding. "That's me." How could I forget?

"How come you don't post anymore?" asks Photo Lens Boy.

People are turning around to look.

"Because"—all of the eyes in the room are now on me—"my parents closed my account."

"Too bad," says the desk-stealer. "But you can still take pictures and share them. Just in a different way."

"True," I say. None of the kids seem to be looking at me funny. In fact, most of the kids are now fiddling with their cameras. They're not really looking at me. I take a

deep breath and try not to think about Snappypic. I try
to be here, right now, in this class.

My Stats:
2 boys who know me from Snappypic
2 girls who sit next to me and are cool
1 pinhole in a box that can capture light
3 dimensions that can be captured in a photo

Mood: Kind of happy to be where I am, right here,
right now. And looking forward to getting crazy on
Crazy Hair Day this coming Monday.

18

That's the Point

As I walk downstairs to breakfast, Mom's phone clatters to the counter. She blinks hard like she is trying to blink away the image of my hair. "Karma. What. Have. You. Done?"

"I've spotted my hair like a cheetah. For Crazy Hair Day."

Dad stands up to inspect and chuckles much too loudly. "Woo-wee. Let's hope it's not permanent." Even Lucky, who hovers by his dog bowl, backs away like I'm a stranger.

"It's temporary." At least that's what it said on the box.

First I sprayed it white-blond with some Halloween dye, then dotted on black spots with a toothbrush dipped in black hair dye.

"You look crazy," says Toby.

"That's the point." I tap my head. "It's Crazy Hair Day today. Remember?"

"Right." Dad taps his balding head. "Guess it would be harder for me to get crazy with this."

"Can I make my hair spotty, too?" asks Toby. "Please? Can I, can I, please?"

I shake my head. "You have to wait until middle school to do something like this."

Toby slumps in his chair. "Not fair. I want crazy hair."

Mom frowns at Dad's phone, which sits on the kitchen table next to his bowl. "You'd think the school would have given the parents some kind of notification or something."

Dad picks up his cell and scrolls through. Since we don't have a home phone anymore, all of the messages go to Dad's phone. "Yup. I see. A message from the school here from last Friday, and also one last night." He shrugs. "No need to read them. Looks like they warned us."

Mom leans over Dad's shoulder. "Hal, thirty-six unread messages? How can you not check your messages?"

"Hey, can you guys take a photo of me?" I ask.

"There's no time," says Mom. "Eat your breakfast quickly. You have five minutes before we have to leave. And Hal"—she turns her head to my dad—"you have fifteen minutes before you take Toby to school."

Dad takes another sip of his coffee. "Yeah, I'm well aware." Normally Mom takes me to school and Dad bikes with Toby to his.

"Are you sure it's called Spirit Week?" asks Toby. "Cause it could be Spiritless Week." He wipes his mouth with the back of his hand. "Get it? Spiritless Week? Where everyone is like this." He flops out of his chair, drops onto the ground with a thud, then drags himself across the floor, yawning. "See, all bored and stuff."

"Like a zombie?" Dad jokes.

"There is no such thing as Spiritless Week." I sigh. Sometimes seven-year-olds can be so silly. I smile. Okay, sometimes silly is good.

> Stressed

As I cross the street on the block before school, I'm suddenly disgusted by how many kids stupidly decided not to do anything for Crazy Hair Day. Volleyball girls pass by me with their long, straight hair pulled into ponytails, and boys with normal crew cuts head into the building.

So much for all of my and Ella's publicity efforts. Well, especially Ella. She was on it all last week. Me, not so much.

Right in front of the school on a big sign in moveable letters, it says:

HAPPY SPIRIT WEEK!

Ethan Loomis slumps by me holding his sax like it weighs a ton, with his regular old look: unwashed, stringy, greasy hair, which is uncrazy and normal for him. And behind him, a whole gaggle of sixth-grade girls are playing with a Magic Eight Ball and not one of them, not a single, solitary one, has done anything remotely crazy about her hair. One girl has pigtails, but just two as opposed to, say, three, four, or five. Had they not seen the Crazy Hair Day posters? Like the one that says *The Eighth Grade Rocks Spirit Week* or Ella's *Get Spirit-erized* poster. Or that giant sign in front of the school?

Were they all not on Snappypic?

Does anybody care?

Did all of the Merton Middle School spirit get sucked into a black hole, and is it alive and well in another normal hair-day galaxy?

Really Crazy

As I shuffle outside the entrance to the school, some boys with regular, mashed-down hair in wool beanies are pointing at me and laughing.

"It's called Crazy Hair Day," I say, pointing to the spots. "So let's not all stare at once."

That's when Ella appears next to our usual meeting spot. She cups her mouth so hard it makes a popping sound. Her eyes widen as she winces. "Did you not get the message?"

"What message?" My heart is starting to pound way too loudly. Because I'm noticing something truly crazy.

"The school changed it," she says. "They made a huge announcement about it on Friday."

"Friday afternoon? That's when I had my orthodontist appointment. How could you not tell me?"

"Well, there were robo calls to parents. My mom got two. I'm *sooo* sorry, Karma. I should have called you, but I just thought you knew."

"Great. My dad never looks at his messages." Behind me I can hear some gasps and giggles.

Ella tilts her head. "Wow. I'm so, so sorry. And of all the days, it had to be picture day."

"Picture day?!!!" Not only am I the one person with polka-dot hair, but it's also the day they take the photos that will be in the yearbook for posterity—and for all time. "This is for real?"

Ella points to the posters taped onto the cinderblock wall. The posters I hadn't noticed until today. It's a photo of a smiling girl and its says:

WEAR YOUR BEST SMILE ☺ TODAY IS PICTURE DAY!

Other kids nearby nudge their friends and point and gawk at me.

"I can't believe this." My heart is pounding. "I'm actually standing around with polka-dot hair. And less than three minutes ago, I thought there was something wrong with everyone else."

Ella's face stretches into a hesitant smile. That's when Auggie Elson and his posse pop up right next to me. He jerks his head around to stare at my polka-dot hair. "Talk about confused. Wow!"

Then he holds up his phone.

A flash fills the hallway and I'm screaming, "Go away!" But it's too late, because Auggie has taken my photo for all of his followers to see.

At this point I consider turning around and running home. My parents would understand.

But no, I can't. Nobody will be there.

"You can borrow my hoodie," says Ella. Then she pulls her phone out of her backpack and glances at it. She gulps hard. "He's already posted it."

I stare at her screen. Then I take a deep breath. "Okay, okay, fine. Someone posted a photo of me. Fine. And that somebody happens to be Auggie. Fine. I can make this better."

Ella bites her lip. "It's pretty bad."

"We can fix this. I just need a phone."

"We should go. So we're not late for advisory." Ella grabs my hand and we rush through the front entrance-way into the school.

"One phone. That's all I need." I stare at Ella plead-ingly. Desperately.

Ella peers down the hallway. "The bell's about to ring."

"I dyed my hair to look like a cheetah. It looks pretty awesome, right?"

"It does," admits Ella hesitantly as kids streaming past do a double take.

"And Crazy Hair Day is Tuesday, so with one phone"—I glance at Ella's pocket—"with your phone, I could recoup. My life could get awesome again. Just give me two minutes."

Ella sighs, looks both ways, and quickly hands me her phone.

I hold it up and take a selfie. "I'm going to make it look like I did it on purpose. A living advertisement for Crazy Hair Day." I hunch over to caption the photo: *I sacrificed my head so the seventh grade could get inspired!* "Tomorrow everyone's going to come to school with spotted hair and it'll be great." I wave Ella's phone. "Woo-hoo! I posted it!"

"Keep it down, Karma."

My eyes glance down at Ella's phone. She has six apps that need updating. "You can set your phone to do this automatically, you know."

"No. Stop, Karma," Ella begs.

My fingers dance on the keyboard. "See, it's already done!"

A walkie-talkie crackles. An official-sounding voice snaps, "Is that a phone, Karma Cooper?"

My Stats:
8 black dots in my hair today
2 bottles of hair dye to color my hair
1 supposed best friend who forgot to tell me *crucial* information

2 parents who failed to check messages

? number of Auggie's followers who will see me during the moment of my *supreme humiliation*. I don't know how many, exactly, but it will be huge.

? About to have my best friend's phone put into cell phone jail

Mood: Extremely flippin' freaked out

19

Bad Hair Day

From the other end of the hall, Mrs. Wallace, the principal, marches right toward me. Students part like the Red Sea. She stares at my polka-dot hair. She stares at my phone. "What's going on here?"

"Um, I'm advertising Crazy Hair Day."

Mrs. Wallace crinkles her face as if she's about to laugh but quickly catches herself. "So you know about the little school rule, right? No phones on campus when school is in session. You heard about that?"

"Um, yeah." My ribs squeeze all the air out of my chest. I'm not sure I'm breathing when I say, "I know about it. But it's not advisory yet, and I was helping people."

Mrs. Wallace furrows her forehead. She runs her hands through her nonspotted blond updo. "I want to hear more about this."

Ella's jaw drops.

And that's when Bailey, Megan, and Janel swish over toward me as I stand there with my polka-dot hair, being drilled by the principal. They're blinking and squinting in confusion.

"I'm—I'm just helping people," I stammer. "I'm advertising Spirit Week. And then I was just . . ."

"You were on your phone," states Mrs. Wallace.

Bailey elbows Megan and Janel.

The warning bell rings.

"Hand it to me," commands Mrs. Wallace in a calm voice.

With my heart pounding, I give her Ella's phone.

Mrs. Wallace sighs deeply. "You've had several warnings, Karma Cooper. You've already had three detentions. You know what this means."

I gasp.

Then Mrs. Wallace examines the phone. A funny look crosses her face. "Hold on. I understand that these days you don't really have a phone." She peers at me intently. "Did you take someone else's?"

"No! I didn't take anybody's. Ella gave me hers. It's very different." And then I clamp my hands over my mouth. Oh, I shouldn't have said that either. Bad Karma. Bad, bad Karma.

Ella's jaw drops farther. Bailey winces.

Mrs. Wallace closes her eyes and shakes her head. She whips out a pink pad and pen from her pocket. "I'm writing you both up." Writing both of us up?

"What's going to happen?" asks Ella. Her face turns pale.

"Well, Ms. Fuentes, your phone will be locked up in the office and you will get a detention." Then she locks eyes with me. "And you, Karma Cooper, will get an in-school suspension."

What?! My parents are going to kill me. "But it was all for a good cause," I protest in one last-ditch effort.

"I appreciate you wanting to be helpful, Karma. But you know the rules and you broke them."

Her usually friendly voice now sounds very official and extremely principal-y. Some kids turn to watch.

I peer over at Ella as Mrs. Wallace clutches her aqua phone with its manga stickers.

Ella blinks so rapidly her mascara smudges. Her eyes are getting red and wet-looking.

"Please don't lock up Ella's phone," I beg. "It's all my fault."

"I'm sorry, but your friend will not get her phone back until she comes to school with her parents and gets a signature to have it released."

Ella gasps loudly. I groan. Ella's mom is going to be sooo mad, not to mention my mom, too. And my dad. My cheeks burn. My arms are shaking.

Mrs. Wallace motions for me to follow her down the hall. "Come with me to the office."

I'm so tremble-y, I'm not sure I can walk.

"We're going to have a little talk with your parents."

This does not get a LIKE at all.

Can It Get Any Worse?

"Dad, I was helping people. Seriously. That's it." We're upstairs in the office atrium next to my parents' bedroom. Earlier we had spent twenty minutes in the principal's office with Mrs. Wallace going over what I had done wrong. I still can't believe she "locked up" Ella's phone *and* that Ella has detention.

Ella's mom is so strict. She'll be ridiculously mad. And now my parents are more than a little bit upset. In-school suspension, the Merton Middle School version of prison, will start tomorrow. I have to do it for two days. Mom sits down next to me on the couch, and Dad leans against the built-in desk across from her. There's no wall behind him since the office is on a mezzanine looking out over the living room.

That means everything being said carries down to the first floor, including the downstairs area where Toby sits, finishing up his snack. He's as silent as a mouse, listening.

"I don't care if you were advertising Crazy Hair Day," Dad booms. "I don't think the principal saw it that way. I don't think they'd have a policy of confiscating a phone if there wasn't a problem!"

"But I was helping. I *promise*." I gaze at Mom pleadingly, but she turns away from me and gets all interested in straightening the magazines on the side table. "Please," I plead. "Please. Didn't you teach me to help others? It's part of having a bat mitzvah. You know—doing good deeds and stuff."

"Are you telling me it was just today?" asks Mom.

That's not a question I want to answer, exactly.

"I might have borrowed Ella's phone a few times, " I admit, "but it was only to help her. She's the cochair of publicity and—"

"Maybe Ella doesn't need your help," Mom points out. "Have you thought about that?"

"That's because . . ." I'm going to tell them about how I don't have time to help Ella because I have so many things to do, but I don't think my parents will understand. "Oh, forget it." Tears tickle my cheeks and I wipe them away furiously.

Dad grabs a pencil off the desk and waves it me. "You didn't listen to our rules, Karma. It was simple. We gave you the pay-as-you go phone and said that if you had good behavior, you could get your real phone back. But sorry, that's not happening."

"As far as I'm concerned, you're going to use the flip phone for the rest of the year," says Mom.

"Unless Karma changes her attitude," says Dad.

"She's not going to change." Mom sighs.

"What? That's not fair," I say. I throw up my hands. "You guys act like I'm evil."

"Not evil," says Mom. "Just out of line."

QUEEN OF LIKES

My Stats:

1 lecture by an angry principal

1 lecture by very angry parents

1 in-school suspension

1 best friend's phone that is also locked up

2 parents who think I'm Bad Karma

Mood: Beyond dismal; cataclysmic

20

> Doomsday Begins

When I get to school, I go to meet Ella at our usual meet-up spot by the water fountain, but she's not there.

Kids with purple and pink hair pass me. Others wear crazy orange wigs with hair that rustles. Oh, Crazy Hair Day. Great. My hair is completely normal when everyone else's is wacked out. I can't win.

On the other side of the quad, Auggie is singing a song he made up about Crazy Hair Day. Justin and Graeme also strum their ukuleles. A small crowd stands in front of them, clapping their hands. I try not to listen.

I glance around the halls looking for Ella. Where is she? She probably double-extra hates me.

And that's when I see Bailey and the Bees standing by the water fountain. There is still no Ella in sight.

Bailey's straight chin-length hair is so jelled it appears wet. Snakelike blue braids stick straight up on Janel's head, and Megan's hair has sprayed-on rainbow colors. They make their way over to me.

Bailey lowers her voice as she pats her crunchy hair. "I still can't believe you got caught by the principal. That was *so* bad."

"I know," I say.

"It's such a bummer you got the in-school suspension. I mean, really. That was super"—Bailey clears her throat as she adjusts her scarf—"harsh."

I swallow hard. "Yeah." I had called Ella last night but she didn't pick up. I'm sure every kid in the school now knows what happened.

"It's probably not the best thing for you to be publicity cochair of the Spirit Week committee. Since you're going to be"—Bailey flinches—"suspended."

"Yeah," I say. "Wouldn't look good, I guess." My heart sinks to my feet. I have just been fired from my first job, and probably from my new group of friends.

"My parents would kill me if I got sent to Mr. Morley," says Megan. "So you're just lucky you're not dead or something." She smiles as if this is the best news ever.

Janel elbows Megan. "Like that's going to make Karma feel better."

"Well, she got caught," says Megan as she opens up a package of gum. She offers it to everyone except me. "And lots of people got in trouble, right?"

My stomach shifts uncomfortably since she, along with Ella and five others, had her phone locked up in the office because of me.

"Ella's super upset with you, Karma," she adds. "She has to get her mom to sign a note to get her phone back."

"I know," I say with a sigh. "But I was trying to help."

"That's exactly what you said to me when you put that chunky peanut butter into my hair," says Bailey.

I wince. "You still remember that?"

She touches her bangs. "My hair only smelled like Jiffy for weeks."

"I put it in to get out the gum."

"Which it didn't do."

"Well, it was supposed to. That was just—"

"Bad luck. Not your fault. I know," says Bailey, and she singsongs *I know* like she knows way too much about me.

That's when Ella brushes past a knot of kids and makes her way over to us. She's got purple sprayed in her hair that's so neon bright I have to blink. But she hasn't changed into her skinny jeans or put on her lip gloss or any mascara. Actually, she's wearing the oversize jeans that she hates. But worst of all, she doesn't say *good morning* in her usual quiet but warm way. Her lips are pressed together in a frown.

My stomach tightens as if there's belt around it.

"Sorry again about your phone," I squeak. "And getting caught." I can tell she's very, *very* mad.

Ella blinks hard and flees into the bathroom. "What's the matter?" I ask, my voice rising. "Did something else happen?"

"You've done enough," says Bailey. The Bees glare at me. I pivot around and go into the bathroom too.

Ella stands in front of the sink, dabbing at her eyes with a balled-up piece of bathroom tissue. Her face is as white as milk. Tears streak down her cheeks.

"Let me make it up to you," I beg.

She glares at me and whispers, "Go away, Karma!"

She thinks she's whispering, but she yells it so loudly that my ears ring.

"What? What else did I do? Whatever it is, I'm sorry!"

Ella shakes her head and waves her hands like she's pushing me away.

So I leave the bathroom and race around the corner to my first in-school suspension.

In-School Suspension

There are only two other people imprisoned with me, two eighth-grade boys who I've never seen before because they rarely come to school when the weather is nice. Mr. Morley, the official jail keeper, scowls at me.

The boy with longer hair yawns every ten seconds.

The one with shorter long hair yawns every five seconds.

This will be my day.

No gym. Or morning break. Or time to chat by the water fountains.

Nothing to do except schoolwork.

Or read a book.

My Hebrew, which I brought with me to school, seems more exciting. I can imagine the singsong chant in my head from that girl on YouTube.

Long Hair is in the bathroom and Longer Hair is going next. The bathroom is attached to the classroom so we don't need to leave.

I want to go to the bathroom in the outside world, and Mr. Morley lets me. Maybe because he feels sorry for me, since he says, "You're not the kind who's usually in my jail." He actually calls it jail.

But he lets me go, and for the first time in a long time, I'm excited about something.

Being excited about going to the bathroom. Really, if you think about it, that's pathetic.

And cursed. Because inside the bathroom is . . . Ella.

Ella

This school has around seven hundred kids. What are the chances that Ella is in the bathroom again? This is *my* chance.

"Ella," I say as she sprays on more purple hair dye. "I get why you're mad, but it was an accident. Please. And if there's something else going on, I want to know."

The spray can fills the room with an ammonia smell and I try not to cough. Ella takes a deep breath and opens her mouth as if she's about to speak. Two sixth graders rush into the bathroom. Ella clamps her mouth shut.

"Ella, I'm worried that your parents went crazy. Tell me what happened."

"I can't," she says as she tucks her bottle of hair dye into her backpack. It's weird but she still she hasn't put on any mascara or lip gloss.

"Please!"

She shakes her head and races out the door.

I stare after her, confused and upset. I slowly walk back to Mr. Morley's room, wondering if I lost my best friend for good.

At Home

I'm back from volunteering at the historical society. At least nobody over there thinks I'm Bad Karma. Anna said I did a great job sorting more photos. It's hard to believe that this Thursday will be my last day volunteering.

I'm sitting on the couch in the family room and Toby's squatting on the floor next to me. He's still got crumbs on his mouth from the donut he ate an hour ago. Dad biked with him to Voodoo Donuts and let him get their most awesome donut, the raspberry jelly–filled one shaped like a little screaming guy and covered with chocolate frosting and a pretzel pin.

I feel the donut voodoo doll's pain. It's almost dinnertime, but I'm not hungry. I think about how the hot dog–eating contest and Crazy Hair Day happened, and I wasn't a part of it. I don't even know who won the Craziest Hair contest or which grade participated the most.

I text in my mind to the patter of the rain hitting the roof: *I know nothing.*

"What are you doing?" asks Toby. He has his box of LEGOs with him. He has all kinds of new pieces because one of mom's friends whose kid graduated college gave away his LEGOs and Toby got all of them. Lots of little yellow pieces that are shaped like little cannons sit in a pile by his feet.

"What are you doing?" asks Toby again.

"I have no idea anymore." My hands flop into my lap, where they look pale and lifeless and useless and silent.

That night I don't get much sleep. My best friend won't speak to me. I have no followers or friends. Maybe someone has made a voodoo doll of me. And that is why everything bad is sticking just like the pretzel in that donut.

My Stats:
1 best friend who UNLIKES me
1 Voodoo donut eaten
1 girl who has no idea how to fix this

Mood: Still beyond dismal

21

Locked Away

Before school starts, before I'm locked away for my last day, I see Bailey getting out of her car by the drop-off circle. The Bees and Ella huddle around Bailey but none of them will look directly at me. They are all dressed in identical white scoop-neck T-shirts and skinny jeans.

I consider saying, *It isn't Quadruplet Day,* but I don't say anything at all.

It's before advisory and I'm standing over by Ella's locker, hoping that she'll speak to me.

So far it's been silence. Ella slams her locker shut. She glares at me. That's just great. Bailey and the Bees approach and circle her like a fence. One of the banners that Ella made is posted next to them. SEVENTH GRADE STAMPS OUT HUNGER. Right now all I want to stamp out is the past two weeks.

Ella whirls around and actually speaks to me. "I'll tell you this much, Karma. You can't be trusted."

Bailey and the Bees nod.

"You spent all of your time worrying about how many followers we had on our Spirit page. Was that really going to help us win the Spirit Stick? And you were constantly borrowing my phone. That was so annoying. You posted comments for me. You LIKED stuff. I know what I like: not you."

"But I was—"

"Helping me?" She shakes her head. "If you haven't noticed, I pretty much ran publicity without you. And made posters, plus decorations. I don't need your help, Karma."

Janel nudges Megan, and Megan nudges Bailey. Nobody has ever seen Ella this mad, including me.

"None of your so-called followers helped," Ella sputters. "We're tied with eighth grade for points for Crazy Hair Day." Then she points down the hallway, near the office where the canned food is stacked. "The eighth grade is way ahead on canned food and the sixth grade is catching up. Today's the final count. You were supposed to tell everybody about the Great Canned Food Sneak Attack, but that didn't happen."

"But I did," I protest. "I let all of our seventh-grade followers know."

"Yeah, but did you ever check to see who followed the page?" asks Bailey. "Lots of those kids don't go to Merton. They just followed it because it was you."

"The sixth graders don't even have Snappypic," says Megan. "Their tower is higher than ours because they passed out fliers on actual paper and because they actually told people in person. You know, word of mouth."

I shrug, even though deep inside I'm feeling more than a little bad. "So old school," I say.

Ella shakes her head. "Well, it worked."

I feel like a creepy statue at a haunted house. Like my body is frozen permanently in a position of humiliating horror. "They picked me because of my followers. Because I'm great at Snappypic. I told them"—I look at the Bees—"I wouldn't do it without you. I made them take you, Ella. They didn't even want you."

Bailey's face turns a shade of red deeper than a fire truck.

Janel blinks in surprise. Megan is still trying to smile.

I tap my chest. "That's why they picked me. Without me," I say, and the words fall out of my mouth like sharp rocks, "you'd be nothing."

Ella stares at me in shock. Her mouth is moving but no words are coming out.

I have gone too far. I know it right away, but I couldn't help it. I was doing all of this for her, in a way. And she didn't even know it. Instead she's making me feel bad. For trying. Trying to do what? To borrow her phone to reach out to people, to be LIKED. And to get her LIKED too.

Ella's eyes water and my stomach turns.

I whisper, "I'm sorry," but it's too late.

She whirls around and flees into the crowded hallway, away from me.

Alone

As I stand there, alone in the crowded hallway, I'm disgusted with myself.

I am not copublicity chair of Spirit Week.

I am not on Snappypic.

I am not LIKED.

I am not really Ella's best friend. Not anymore.

When I was little, I remember thinking on the very last day of first grade in Mrs. Fitch's class, *I am not a first grader.*

But then during the summer I wasn't quite a second grader yet, either.

So then I thought—*I am not a second grader.*

The summer was the time in between being something.

But this isn't summer. It's March, and yet I feel like I'm in between being one thing and something else. For a moment I think about my bat mitzvah reading. Moses left the palace but he had something else better to do.

I just don't know what that something else is yet.

I've got to be in the suspension room in five minutes. The bell is about to ring and my jail is located in a completely different wing of the school. Right now I'm at school with everyone else but I'm completely alone.

No Snappypic.

No followers.

No friends. Actual friends.

And this is when Milton P. decides to march up to me.

Bad Timing

"Hell-o, Karma," Milton P. says in his slightly robot-y voice. "I agree with you about the Millennium Falcon. Do you want to discuss this?"

I throw up my hands, screaming, "I do not want to discuss LEGOs, Milton P. I do not like LEGOs. Go away!" I swing my hand toward him, and his shoe box goes flying.

We all watch in horror as it launches into the air like a real spaceship, only a real spaceship lands; it has landing gear and falls safely into the ocean.

But what falls out of the shoe box has no landing gear. And actually, it *is* a spaceship. A LEGO spaceship, a complicated one like the ones Toby makes, falls out of the box and splinters into what seems like a thousand pieces.

That's what's inside the mysterious shoe box? I feel like screaming to Ella, "Come look!" But of course I can't do that.

Milton P. looks so astonished, not in a spy way, but in a real-person way—a regular kid who has lost something special to him. I know that feeling.

Bug, one of Milton P.'s semifriends, lunges over,

screaming, "Dude, what did you do to him?! Dude, that was given to him by his *dad*!"

Milton P. is sitting, crying, his nose running, curled up over his LEGO pieces.

Oh. Wow. I feel. Extra. Hugely. Terrible.

I've done a lot of bad things.

But this may be the worst.

As Milton P. looks at his LEGOs spread across the floor of the Merton Middle School hallway, he opens his mouth and bellows.

> Never

Milton P. will never speak to me again, and I will probably never speak to Auggie or Ella or Bailey or Megan or Janel ever again. And Milton P., even though I told him that I'd fix the Millennium Falcon model. Even though I told him I'd buy him a thousand model spaceships.

> Walking

I'm dragging myself home, dazed and upset, when I spot Annette Black practically skipping on the other side of the street. When I was little, she was my favorite baby-sitter ever. She showed me how to do a perfect handstand and she's the one who first showed me Snappypic.

She waves at me and gives me a big smile as she crosses the street. She's one of the smiley-est people I know. "What's going on?" she asks as she heads over to me. "I haven't seen you at religious school in such a long time." She bounces toward me like she might do a cartwheel. "We miss you. Especially the kindergartners." Last year in sixth grade, I used to help out with little kids at my synagogue.

I shrug. "I've just been so busy. Soccer. Studying for my bat mitzvah."

"Don't you have over ten thousand followers on Snappypic?"

My throat squeezes so tightly that I can't get a full breath. I can't bring myself to tell her I have zero followers right now, along with everything else that stupid phone and site have cost me at this point.

"Well, you beat me." Her blond ponytail flips in the air as she shakes her head. "I'm not really doing that anymore. Snappypic, I mean. I slowed down in high school. This year I'm taking three AP classes. I'm editor of the paper and on the cheer squad, so I'm doing a ton of stuff I like."

"That's cool," I say. Rain starts to drizzle down now. I grab my jacket out of my backpack and stuff my camera into a waterproof pocket.

Annette pops open an umbrella. "Your photos are so good. The ones I've seen on Snappypic."

I swallow hard and confess. "My parents closed my account."

"Oh, that's too bad." She pats my shoulder. "You'll figure out something awesome to do. It's really good to see you." The driving rain plasters her hair against her face.

"You too." More and more water pours out of the sky. I push my hood farther over my eyes as I dodge a puddle that's forming on the sidewalk. And then I think maybe I had already figured out awesome things to do. And maybe, just maybe, I was doing them already.

My Stats:
400 pieces of LEGOs spread in the hallway
1 former best friend who is very, very loud about her madness at me
0 things to LIKE right now
2 hands free to start making something awesome

Mood: No longer surprised by anything

22

What Is Time?

Toby and I lay down on our stomachs on the family room floor. He has been showing me how LEGOs fit together and how you follow the directions, step by step. It's sort of like photography. At least that's what Ren was saying today in class. We learned all about depth of field and how you can focus on just one thing that counts.

Well, I know what I'm going to focus on right now—rebuilding Milton's LEGO ship. Unfortunately, rebuilding my friendship with Ella won't be as easy.

For my Milton P. project, I already have the LEGOs.

Bins and bins of them. Toby said I could have as many as I wanted. I realize that I can't put these LEGOs together in a way that will look like Milton P.'s Millennium Falcon, but I can make something spaceship-ish. Something cool.

Toby says to me, "It's six eighty-six. We get to eat a snack."

"There's no such time as six eighty-six."

Toby breaks out laughing. "What's worse, having no time or too much time?"

That's something I don't really know.

Hebrew Trickles Down

I go upstairs to start practicing Hebrew. I'm going to try to be good. I lower my voice and go over a prayer before I read the *haftarah*, a reading following my Torah portion about Moses. Somehow when I chant it, with the rain softly pattering outside, everything falls into place. I don't stumble. I lick my lips and chant it again, only this time a little more loudly and a little more confidently.

Later when I go downstairs to see if I can help with dinner, Mom says, "I could hear you up there, Karma. You're sounding good."

Dad stands in the kitchen slicing up some potatoes. Toby works next to him and is placing the already cut-up potatoes onto a tray.

Mom is pulling some chicken breasts out of the fridge. "You were up there for a long time," she says, smiling.

"Can I help?" I ask.

"Sure," says Mom. "You can clear the table later and load the dishwasher."

"All right." Not my favorite jobs. But I'm not going to complain.

"Keep up the good work with your Hebrew," says Dad as he sets the cutting board into the sink.

I grab my camera and step outside, even though it's just started to lightly rain again and there's not much light out. I can't wait to see what I'll find.

Bigger

It's right before bedtime, and Toby curls next to me on my bed. "What finger is bigger?" Toby shoves his hand into my face and points to his ring and index fingers.

It's weird but they're the same.

"Are they supposed to be the same?" he asks in a worried voice.

I look at my own hand. My pointer finger is longer. "I don't think it matters."

I grab the camera and take a close-up of Toby's strange but cool same-size fingers. "It's okay to be different," I say.

Actually, that was my second post after the gopher incident. I had used it to match an image of a bunny with misshapen ears. I chose it to go with the photo because it was cute. Because I thought I could get a lot of followers. But now I'm saying it only for Toby, and I get to see a real honest-to-goodness face afterward with a big smile.

My Stats:
400 pieces of LEGOs spread in my own family room
1 awesome little brother who shows me how to build
2 hands that made my first major LEGO project

Mood: Pretty ok! But missing my best friend still . . .

23

What About Auggie?

"I've gotten three hundred new followers this week," Auggie brags as I pass him in the hallway. I'm on my way to the cafeteria. I'm happy about being out of the school jail but I'm not happy about probably eating by myself.

"You can check it out," says Auggie. Today is Wear Your School Colors Day, and Auggie, like almost everyone else, is dressed in blue and orange. "Did you hear me?" he asks.

"Uh-huh," I say, scoping out a table.

"And I've just won an Olympic medal in dog sledding."

"Uh-huh."

"And I just turned into a zombie."

"Uh-huh."

"You don't care," he says. "Is something wrong?" he asks, although he knows. Everyone knows.

"No," I say. "Nothing is wrong." I'm much too good at lying. I'm going to have to do something about this.

Milton P. Approaches

I stroll into the cafeteria and see Ella, Bailey, Megan, and Janel. They're all clustered together, laughing hysterically. After my outburst, I can't sit with them. I gaze around. Milton P. eats with his friends. He's wearing his thick belt and bending down to sip a straw without holding it.

I stride across the lunchroom with a surprise gift in my hands. Some kids turn around to look at me. Bailey glances over at me. Her eyebrows scrunch together like she's trying to figure something out. The rest of the kids in the caf are holding a collective breath as I look over at

Milton P. and say the craziest thing I've ever said: "I built this LEGO for you, to look like your dad's."

Milton P. blinks at it. "It's really terrible."

"I know, but I tried, really." I take a step backward.

"Don't be sorry." He swallows. "It was a nice thing to do." Then Milton P. pats the empty chair next to him. "You can sit with us."

"Okay," I say.

During lunch, I take out my dad's camera. Well, my camera now. Mostly Milton P. ignores me. He eats his food and fiddles with the LEGO I made him. His friends barely grunt. But that's okay. Using the telephoto lens, I take photos of things around the cafeteria. The tacos, the wilted chopped lettuce. And people, too, like Milton P., in an unguarded, real moment as he examines his new LEGO.

A photo of Bailey singing a scale.

Janel dancing in a chair.

Lia Clark swinging her clarinet case and eating a muffin.

Ella drawing.

Megan going over stuff with volunteers for the Spirit Week dance tomorrow. And it's so cool. Just to watch. Just to wait. Just to snap what I like.

More Milton P.

In the hallway during second break, Milton P. shuffles up to me and shows me a small spacecraft. "You like it, right?" He points at me. His finger is so close it's practically in my nostril. I'm laughing and nodding even though I have no idea what he is talking about.

"I call it the TI-300," says Milton P. "It doesn't appear to have enough power. But you see, I did it again. I have a hidden energy source in the cockpit." He's all red and beaming and proud of himself as he holds out the little LEGO spaceship, the one I made him. He may look odd, but I notice he smells nice, like chocolate and rain.

"Do you want to take a photo of it?" He points to the LEGO. "You know, with your camera?"

I smile. "One step ahead of you, Milton P. Already did."

"Cool," he says.

"Yeah," I say. "Cool."

I Take Photos of a Chip

After school, using a shallow depth of field, I take photos of old crayons with peeling labels that are spread

out on the desk in my room. I look up and gaze out
my bay window. The trees sway and bow in the wind.
The clouds hang low, puffy and gray. Pointing my camera upward, I shoot just the edges where the soggy sky
touches the bright green of the pine trees.

By now, I've snapped more than five hundred pictures in just over two weeks. Give me a few months and
I'll take thousands!

It's so fun playing with focal length. I take a bunch
of photos of a tortilla chip, so close that you can see
the bubbles and hills and spice, but not the edges of the
chip itself. I wish I could post it on Snappypic and write,
Guess what? But for now it's my private treasure.

I go upstairs to the family computer and look at
all of the historical society photos I've taken. I upload
them onto a slideshow site that I like. After a quick
snack, I bike over to the historical society as it softly
drizzles outside.

I can't believe it's my last day there. I sure hope
they like my images. I want to share them right away
but decide to wait. After two hours quickly pass, I'm
finishing up sorting photos of old farms and stuff
when Dorina, Karen, and Anna walk up to me. I gaze

up at the clock on the wall above the bulletin board. It's time to go.

"I can't believe how time has flown," murmurs Dorina. "It feels like you just started your community service project, and now you're done." She shakes her head. I think her bouffant hairdo looks especially beautiful right now in the muted late afternoon light.

"We have a surprise for you," says Anna.

"Oh? What?" I sit up straighter, wondering what it could be.

"Well," Anna glances backs at the stairs. "We have to wait for Neda. She's still on the phone."

"Okay," I say. "While we wait, I have something to show you." I gesture to Anna's desk, which like always is filled with stacks of file folders. "Can I use your computer?"

Her eyes curious, Anna smiles. "Of course."

Everyone gathers round, and I get to the slideshow site where I've uploaded all of the photos. "Okay, ta-da!" I announce. The images of all the volunteers flash onscreen, as well as all kinds of shots inside the building. The close-up of the gleaming white gloves. The labels with beautiful calligraphy on the ephemera boxes. And tons of shots of the staff and volunteers. Karen trying on her fluffy pink boa. There're *ohh*s and *ahh*s.

"Hey, that's me," says Dorina, pointing to the one of her pulling out the photo books. "When did you sneak in that shot?"

"I have my ways," I say mysteriously.

Someone clicks up to us in high heels from the stairs. I twist around to look. It's Neda, of course. She leans over Anna's shoulder to look. "Wow. Those are really good, Karma." I glance back. Her owlish eyes grow even bigger behind her black oval frames. "You know that slideshow we have downstairs in the lobby sitting area?" she asks.

I nod.

"Well, it's been running forever. I think we could show this in the lobby."

"That's a great idea," says Anna. Both Dorina and Karen nod in agreement.

"Really?" I say.

Neda pushes up her glasses. "Yes. Definitely."

I peer over at Dorina, Karen, and Anna. "So was that the surprise, then?"

Anna shakes her head. "No, that would be impossible.

We didn't know you had a slideshow for us. Those photos were your surprise."

"I guess that was my thank-you. You know, for letting me volunteer here." I gaze at everyone crowding around the computer. "And showing me stuff. It's been really . . . cool."

"Maybe you're a future librarian in the making," suggests Karen.

"Maybe," I say.

"You've done a good job with the sorting." Anna glances at the stacks of photos that I've made.

"And I appreciate the care you've exercised in handling the photos," says Neda. Her eyebrows rise in a question. "What if it wasn't your last day with us?"

"Really? I could keep on coming in?" I bounce in the chair.

Neda, Anna, Dorina, and Karen all say yes at the same time.

Neda steeples her fingers. "Great! I have a special assignment for you, then." She looks at me expectedly. "We've gotten a grant to do an oral history of the synagogue. It was constructed in 1956 and we're interviewing the founders. Eight of the twelve are still living, so it's important to do this." She pauses. "We'd like for you to take the photos."

"Me? A kid?"

Dorina folds her arms. "There's nothing you can't do if you put your mind to it." Everyone's nodding.

"We were hoping you'd want to stay on, and we'd talked about a possible project," says Anna.

"So this is the surprise? This is what you all were talking about?"

Anna spreads her arms in a flourish. "Yes!"

Everyone wears big smiles.

"That's awesome," I gush. "I'd love to photograph all of the founders."

"We thought you could start with the Steinbergs since both of them were presidents of the temple in the early years," explains Neda.

"Hey, wait a minute! I know them!" I say excitedly. "I just spoke with Mrs. Steinberg at Milton P.'s bar mitzvah."

"Yes, I was there too," says Neda, as if I need reminding. For a minute, I think she's mad, but she's still smiling. "We'd like you to find an adult mentor who could give you some guidance. I can make a recommendation." She gives Dorina a meaningful look.

Dorina taps her sweater-vest. "Me."

"Wow." I smile. "I'd really like that."

An Allowance

When I get home, I tell my family all about the oral history project, and how I'm going to continue volunteering at the historical society. My mom and dad are so excited that they call my grandparents in New Jersey to tell them about it. Toby asks me if I will give him my autograph, which is pretty funny.

"Hysterical," I say.

"You will be historical," says Dad.

Then Mom asks me why I don't invite Ella over to celebrate. She wants to take everyone out for smoothies. But I tell her that's okay.

She studies my face. "Is everything all right between the two of you? I haven't seen her around."

And that's when I break down and tell Mom and Dad everything that is going on. How I have no friends. How Ella won't speak to me and I won't speak to her and how having Snappypic made me feel special. I cry and cry and Mom strokes my hair and tells me that it will get better. Dad hugs me, and Mom and Toby hug me too. It's a quadruplet hug.

> Toby Has a Confession

After dinner, I go upstairs to my bedroom and Toby wanders over, shifting from foot to foot like maybe he's got to pee.

"What's the matter, Tobs?"

He sits down next to me on my bed. "I should have told you." He presses his knees to his forehead, rocking back and forth on the couch.

"Told me what?"

He kicks a balloon with his bare toes. "I know where they hid your phone."

"What? How do you know?"

"Because"—he swallows—"I found it and used it."

"What?!" I slam my book down. "Toby, you took my phone? Really?"

He doesn't answer and continues to bat the balloon with his feet.

"I'm not mad," I lie. "Just tell me where you found it."

I hope my voice sounds light, sweet, and carefree.

"In Mom's sock drawer. In the very back."

Toby grips the knotted part of the balloon with his dirty toes.

"Why didn't you tell me you found it?"

As Toby rocks back and forth, Lucky trots over and licks him.

"What did you do on my phone?"

He rolls over onto his stomach. "I figured out how to talk to people. But first I charged it up."

"People? What people? Who did you talk to, Toby?"

He shrugs. "He sent me photos of his LEGOs. And I told him how much I liked them, only I didn't know how to send him back photos. His name is Milton P."

"You have been texting Milton P.? Oh my gosh!"

And then I remember that last year I was in a social studies project with him and everyone in the group exchanged numbers and I put it into my phone.

I grab Toby's balloon away. So that was why Milton P. thought I loved LEGOs. He wasn't just making it up. He thought Toby was me. I stomp on the balloon so it pops in one loud burst.

"Ow! Ow! Ow!" screams Toby as though he's the one who was popped.

"What's going on up there?" asks Mom.

"Nothing!" I shout. This is not something I want her to know about.

"You popped my balloon," Toby says in a small voice. "How could you?"

He looks at me, his eyes big and watery. "Because I wanted to be just like you."

Like me? What? Why would he want to be like . . . and then I catch my breath and look at him with his dirty toes, staring at the pieces of red balloon on his floor. "I'm sorry," I apologize. I give Toby a hug before he scampers out.

I pace around the room. I have to tell Milton P. that it's not me. It explains everything, of course. Milton P.'s comments about LEGOs that made *absolutely* no sense at all.

I'd tell him the truth. That it was my seven-year-old brother.

And then a funny thought occurs to me. I'm not even going to look in that sock drawer for my phone, even if a part of me really, really wants to do it.

My Stats:
1 oral history photography project

QUEEN OF LIKES

1 quadruplet hug
1 camera in a sock drawer waiting to be found
1 little brother who wants to be just like me

Mood: Like a roller coaster, up and down

24

Where's Milton P.?

On the day of the Spirit Rally, I bring my camera to school and take photos.

I snap shots of Bailey singing and Megan sharing gum and Ella sketching (she gives me a weird look) and Milton P. playing with LEGOs and anything else cool. I also take photos of some rose bushes all pruned back outside the front office with the light all lovely and filtered in the background, and the cracked cement with a dandelion growing out of it.

I seek out Milton P. "Is this Milton P.'s locker?" I ask a girl with one long braid.

"Unfortunately," she says, twirling her combination. I wait until Milton P. arrives.

"I have something to tell you, Milton P.," I say. "It's about the texts I've been sending you. There is something you need to know."

Milton P.'s grin stretches across his face so wide it looks like his skin might pop. His freckles are almost dancing on his nose. "I like texting you. I think you are the only person in the seventh grade who knows almost as much as me about LEGOs."

Then it hits me. That text the morning after my phone was taken away, when my phone was stuffed in the dresser: It was Milton P.

"We've been texting a while, huh?" I say. "For a few weeks?"

"Sounds right." Then he smiles a gummy smile and his outer-space eyes twinkle. "That's so weird you have something to tell me. Because I have something to tell you. Well, show you. Close your eyes and count. Now say *Star Wars* three times."

I sigh and the girl twirling her combination shrugs her shoulders and sashays down the crowded hallway. Kids begin to crowd the hallway as first break is almost ending. "Stars Wars Star Wars Star Wars," I chant.

"Okay," says Milton P. "Now open your eyes."

I open them and Milton P. whips his hands into his shoe box and then pulls out something that flashes. It's shaped like a giant cell phone but it's made mostly from LEGOs. "I heard yours got taken away so I made this for you."

It's got a panel of buttons and a little screen, and I can't help it—I gasp. "This is a-mazing, Milton P."

"That's not all. Touch it."

My fingers graze the buttons.

"No, really punch it."

A light flashes. "How did you do this?"

"Special parts. I had to order it off this site I found out about and . . ."

I lean forward and hug, actually *hug,* Milton P. Daniels. This is about the nicest thing anyone has ever done for me, ever.

Ella strolls toward us with Bailey and the Bees. They're only about twenty feet away. Ella stares at me. She stares at Milton P. Everyone's mouths drop open. I expect Megan to say, "This can't be happening, right?"

I expect Bailey and Janel to shake their heads and turn their backs.

I expect Ella to race away from us as if we are

standing at the center of a nuclear contamination site. But nobody is doing any of that.

Instead Ella is clapping. "Way to go, Milton P.!"

Not "Snollygoster." Not "Thing."

Just at that moment Auggie waltzes by and whistles. "Looks like Milton P. has it going on. I'm jealous." And then there is a chorus of *ewws*. Auggie takes a photo of us. "I'm posting this to Snappypic!"

But I don't look up. I don't care. I'm just staring at the LEGO phone. "It's awesome, really."

Milton P. peers at me through his darkened glasses. "And what was it that you wanted to tell me? About the text messages. I mean, they were a little weird. Sometimes you sounded like a little kid. I thought you might have been sneaking your phone and didn't have enough time to type.

"Oh, the messages. Right. I want to tell you that . . . I meant everything I said to you. That you're an amazing LEGO builder and don't ever stop building. Ever!"

The Rally

In the gym after fifth period everyone sits on the bleachers with their grades. Lots of boys and a few girls have painted their faces half blue and half orange. It's a sea of colors.

I sit in the bleachers by myself in the back. Bailey and the Bees and Ella sit in the front of the seventh-grade section. Across the way, the eighth graders sit. The sixth graders all congregate in a group to our left but on the same side of the gym. Lots of kids wear school T-shirts. There's a yellow shirt with a dolphin that says PROUD TO BE A MERTON DOLPHIN. Milton P. sits in the second row with his friends. He turns around and waves at me. I wave back.

Mrs. Grayson gets up to speak and talks about how wonderful this week is and starts reading quotes about Spirit Week. "We asked the question, What does Spirit Week mean to you? Here are some of the responses." Mrs. Grayson clears her throat. "Lexi Granger wrote, 'Spirit Week means middle-school spirit.' So true!"

Well, obviously, since this is a middle school and not an elementary school or high school or nursery school.

Everyone claps for the quote. Lexi Granger blushes and waves her hands at everyone like she's a princess at a parade.

"Jordan Garcia says 'It's a whole week of fun!' I certainly agree!" adds Mrs. Grayson.

Fun for some people.

The more I think about fun, the more I look at the clock.

Two twenty. Ten more minutes. Then I can walk home with my camera, taking more pictures.

"The purpose of Spirit Week is to get everyone enthused and supportive of our school." Mrs. Grayson gazes at the bleachers and shields her eyes like the sun is in them. Only it's inside a gym and it's drizzling outside. "Who's got spirit? Can't hear you, Dolphins. Who's got spirit?"

"We do!" shout some kids.

Mrs. Grayson lifts her arms like a conductor. "Can't hear you!"

"We do!" Everyone screams in a deafening roar. And that's when Janel hops down onto the gym floor and cues the seventh grade to do their dance move. A hop and a wiggle. Only half the class does it.

Ten more minutes. The clock is slowing down. Or maybe there has been a power outage because I'm sure that five minutes have gone by and not just one minute. "Now some words from Merton's principal, Mrs. Wallace." Mrs. Grayson steps away from the mic.

"This week serves to get people involved, working cooperatively and united in a common goal of promoting our school," says Mrs. Wallace. "And this is when one of the grades will win the Spirit Stick!"

I glance toward Bailey and watch her hug Ella, and Ella hugs her back and they're all eagerly waiting. I am too.

As if she can read my mind, Mrs. Wallace says, "We'll find out who wins the Spirit Stick in a moment, but first let's have our fall sports teams down here."

I'm back to looking at the clock as the football team and the tennis team and the volleyball team and the cross-country team make it to the gym floor.

Everyone hollers.

And then Mrs. Wallace says, "Let's hear it, sixth grade." She holds up something that looks like a stake wrapped in blue-and-orange tape.

The sixth grade cheers and bangs their feet on the bleachers.

"Not bad," shouts Mrs. Wallace at the top of her lungs into the microphone. "Can you outdo that, seventh grade?"

The seventh grade holds up even more signs, and shouts and pounds on the bleachers so its sounds like thunder.

"Pretty good. Eighth grade, can you top that?" She points the Spirit Stick at the eighth grade. Auggie has a horn and it's so loud that it hurts my ears, but there's not as much clapping. Still Mrs. Wallace goes, "I think the eighth graders might have it." The sixth graders and the seventh graders boo. Lily Pommard turns to Auggie and starts high-fiving him.

The eighth graders have once again won the Spirit Stick. No. Please. No.

"However, I can't be sure," says Mrs. Wallace. "Let's do it one more time. But all at once."

So because of the thunderous stomping feet and screams and whistles, there's no way to really tell who's making the most noise, but Mrs. Wallace keeps on pointing. She goes from the seventh to the eighth grade and then points at the sixth and then back to the eighth, where Auggie is yelling through his megaphone.

"Okay." Mrs. Wallace motions for us to keep quiet.

She takes the Spirit Stick and points not at the eighth grade, not to the seventh grade . . . but at the sixth grade.

What? This is a snapshot in my mind I do not want to take. The sixth graders are going crazy. They are running on the gym floor. Gina, the sixth-grade leader, is throwing candy. The kids are jumping up and down. Some are even doing handstands and shouting, "Pizza! Ice cream! Pizza! Ice cream!"

Meanwhile, the seventh graders around me gasp and moan. Janel, Bailey, Megan, and Ella all console each other with a giant hug. Across the gym, the eighth graders whisper to each other furiously. Some shake their heads or put their arms in front of their chests in a we-were-robbed posture. Lily Pommard looks like she's crying.

I know exactly how she feels.

Clapping, Mrs. Wallace says, "First I want to commend all the grades for their participation. And a special recognition to Auggie Elson for personally collecting three hundred and thirty-two cans for the food bank. And I also want to especially thank the seventh grade for sponsoring the dance this year. Together, all of you have contributed to an outstanding Spirit Week!"

In the front row, the Bees give each other a significant look. Really. Sixth graders!

"It's never happened before," says a boy in front of me with a crew cut. I think his name is Charlie.

"I can't believe it," says his friend.

"It's because of that exchange student. He won the hot dog–eating contest by a long shot and he happens to be a sixth grader. Even though, technically, I think the guy should be an eighth grader."

All kinds of comments surround me. We lost. But the eighth grade lost too. Suddenly, from across the gym, I feel Auggie's stare. He mouths, "Too bad," and shrugs.

I mouth back, "I know." Ella turns around and our eyes meet. She sees me looking at Auggie and Auggie looking at me. And now I'm making a face at him.

And he's making a face at me. And we're both sort of laughing.

I thought he would be superangry at losing, but he doesn't look that mad. And neither am I.

Auggie throws his cardboard megaphone into the air.

Sometimes life is stranger than any book or movie or TV show.

Even Stranger

The amazing thing is that right after school, Dad lets me go to the drugstore and make a disc of all my photos and download them onto his laptop. Then I make some photo posters.

Later I'm nibbling on some pumpkin seeds when Toby dramatically flops on the couch in the family room. "What's the matter?" I ask.

He moans. "Bryce is sick. He was supposed to come

over today. It's not fair." He slumps down further on the couch. "Nothing in my life is going the right way." I know the feeling, but I don't say this out loud.

"C'mon. We're going to the park. We'll take Lucky for a walk." At the mention of his name, Lucky pops out of his dog bed.

Toby's forehead crinkles. "We are?" He peers outside. "It's raining."

"So? When has that ever stopped us?"

I grab our raincoats and snap on Lucky's leash. We bike to the park with Lucky and I put down my hood, tucking my camera on the inside of my coat. Fat raindrops slide down my cheek and slip down my neck.

Taking out my camera, I stand under a shelter. Toby jumps in even more puddles. It's just a light drizzle now. I play with distance. I put the soccer ball down and focus on him, messing with the depth of field. That's moving around the aperture, which is the opening and closing of the lens. The background is blurry and only the soccer ball is in focus. Then I adjust the aperture some more. Each time I snap, the background becomes sharper and sharper. On the next nondrizzle day, I want to take a photo of the moon as it rises over Mount

Hood. I'd make the moon clear and the snow-capped mountain dreamlike in the background.

"What are you doing?" asks Toby.

"Nothing."

"I want to do nothing."

"I've got an idea." I direct Toby to jump and take photos of him. Playing around again with the depth of field, I decide I like it best when I can focus on Toby and everything in the background goes blurry. I focus on what's important, what's right in front of me.

What's Farther Away?

On the way back I spot Ella riding her bike on the path by the grove of trees inside the park. From across the street I see that she's got on her backpack and she's riding toward the school. I tell Toby to go home with Lucky and that I will be back soon. I suddenly, urgently need to talk to Ella. On my bike, I race back to the park to catch up.

The sun stretches through the clouds even though it's misting.

It's so beautiful I want to take a photo.

But I don't have time.

There's a dad kicking a soccer ball to his kid and an older lady walking her yappy little dogs. They bark at a jogger as she passes by.

"No, Fifi," the lady says in a tiny little voice, like she's talking to a little kid.

I see Ella. Yes, I beat her. I figure she has to hop off her bike and walk around the puddles. But she stays on her bike as she passes the little dogs that look like stuffed animals but think they are wolves.

Fifi lunges for Ella's tire.

"No, Fifi," says the lady in her small voice.

She's so busy saying no to Fifi that the other dog, who she calls Muffin, is growling at Ella.

"Hey!" I call out, but it's too late.

Ella's bike swerves, skidding on a rock. She puts her feet down just in time. "I almost ran over your dog," she says, out of breath.

The lady steps daintily down the path and picks up her dog. It's still barking and growling. "You should go slower."

"They need to go to obedience school or something," snaps Ella. She glances over at me but doesn't wave.

"We're working on that." The lady murmurs

something like "Bad Muffin" to her dog, and then strides away with the two dogs yanking on their leashes, desperate to attack Ella.

Ella pedals away hard but her bike is turned funny. She's got her head down and her bike gets stuck in a puddle. She flies off the bike. It slaps on top of her. Her backpack flips upside down. Colored pens and art things tumble into the mud.

I pedal up to Ella. "Are you okay?" I hop off my bike and lift hers off of her. "Those dogs should be registered lethal weapons."

Ella winces as she tries to stands up, and immediately falls back down.

"Are you okay?" I ask.

"My ankle. I can't put any weight on it."

"Maybe you sprained it." I collect all her drawing pads, wipe them off as best I can, and stick them inside her backpack.

She glances at her bike. The gears are off the chains and she's rubbing her ankle. "It really hurts." She grimaces.

"It could be broken. Here, lean on me and we can hop to my house."

Ella shakes her head. "I can't. I'm supposed to be

decorating the gym. Right now. I'm seven minutes late."
She looks down toward her pocket. "Where's my phone?"

Then her eyes travel two feet ahead. And my eyes
travel two feet ahead. And there is her phone, or at least
what was her phone. The screen is so shattered it looks
like a spiderweb. "I can't believe this! My mom's going
to kill me."

"Maybe just the screen's broken." I pick it up and
push on the button. Miraculously, her phone turns on.
"See, it's fine."

But Ella's not smiling. She's sort of sniffling as she
points to something across from the rock. It's a mud
puddle, and inside of it sit all of the stars and moons
that Ella has made. They are normal-looking, just like I
suggested. Rolls of yellow streamers, out of their plastic
bags, are also sopping wet.

"Oh no!" she cries.

"Maybe they can dry," I say.

Ella blinks back tears. "The dance starts in three
hours. We started decorating yesterday afternoon, but
these are the finishing touches. Everything is ruined."

Ella hobbles toward the decorations, grimacing.
"Oh my gosh. I can't believe this!"

"Let's make sure you're okay first and then worry

about the decorations," I say. The rain hisses and fat drops splash onto my cheek. "We should call your parents."

Tears flow out of Ella's eyes. "We can't. My dad's away on a trip. He's in Phoenix. And my mom is at the gym. So she won't even pick up." Ella's face is streaked with mud and rain and tears. She sniffles and wipes her eyes on her sleeve. She's wearing a nice dress for the dance. Or, it was nice.

"I'll call my dad," I say in a hopeful voice. "He's home and only a few houses away. He'll come with the car." I take Ella's phone, since I left Flippie at home, and call.

"Sorry," says Ella, even as she winces.

"For what?"

"For not . . . being there."

"It's okay, I get it."

I really, really, really want to ask Ella about what happened earlier. Why she was so upset in the bathroom, but it isn't the right moment.

So I call my dad and he immediately answers. "Dad," I say. "It's Karma."

"What's wrong?" asks Dad.

"I'm in the park. Ella fell. She might have broken her ankle or something. She was on her bike and her parents aren't home. . . ."

Dad tells me he'll be right over, and that Mom's home and will stay with Toby.

"He'll be here in three minutes," I say as I collect the wet decorations and dump them in a nearby trash can.

"I knew already," Ella whispers.

"What? That my dad could come?"

She shakes her head. "The only reason I'm cochair was because of you."

"What are you talking about? That's not true."

"What you said on Monday. It was all true. *You're* the one they wanted. They knew you could get everyone involved. I'm just good with colored pencils."

"You're not just good. You're amazing. You're the best. You're professional," I argue. "What's crazy is thinking that Bailey and the Bees wouldn't get right away how awesome you are. You didn't even need me as cochair. I probably just made everything worse."

"That's not completely true. Okay, maybe, kind of." Smiling weakly, Ella stands up and limps toward her bike. "Ow," she groans.

"Don't try to move, Ella. You could do some serious damage."

Ella wipes her eyes. "I hate being mad at you. Really, really hate it."

"And I wish I had borrowed someone else's phone, like Auggie's. So his would have been locked up, not yours, and we wouldn't have this fight," I reply.

"Speaking of which, he's been driving me crazy asking about you, Karma."

"Why? Because he wants to hear the details of my lock-up?"

Ella shakes her head. "It's more like he's obsessed with you. Have you noticed he can't stop looking at you?"

"Me?"

"Yeah."

"He's just an insensitive, annoying, hyper ukulele-playing pest. He's waiting to figure out when he can photo bomb me next."

"Hello." Ella waves her hand in my face. "Are you dumb? Auggie likes you."

"What? He hates me."

"Then why did he ask me when the invitations to your bat mitzvah are coming? Huh? And whether he's invited and whether there's going to be a party?" A huge grin spreads across Ella's face. "And if you were coming to the Spirit Dance tonight?" Nobody asks people to dances at Merton, but if someone asks about you, then it usually means that they will ask you to dance a slow dance.

"Really? REALLY?" I close my eyes and imagine Auggie as someone who would want to dance with me. And as someone danceable. And I kind of almost see it. Maybe the same way that Ella can see the cuteness in Milton P. "So I guess there are some things I don't get."

Ella's smile gets even bigger, if that's possible. "Me too," she agrees.

"Like Milton P. is not a spy. He's just a boy."

"Yeah, a strange but cute boy," says Ella. "So you know that Auggie posted a video called 'The Girl with Leopard Hair'? It's got that photo of you and he's strumming his ukulele."

"What?" It's like I've been living on another planet—my own life. "Do I want to know?"

Ella picks up her phone, thumbs through it, and hands it to me. The song is about a girl who wakes up with spots all over her hair, and how it's school picture day. I'm popping my hand over my open mouth because I can't believe he's done it.

And it's really catchy, actually, and kind of sweet.

That cute girl with spots and dots all over town!

Ella gazes down. "Three hundred and thirty-three LIKES."

I stare at the video of Auggie in his brown-and-white

spotted beanie playing his orange ukulele and singing about a gutsy girl with leopard-striped hair. And suddenly I'm realizing what this means.

This is all weird for me. Ella and I are giggling like mad, and that's when Dad comes up with his car.

"I thought someone was hurt," says Dad.

"She is," I say, nodding at Ella.

Dad shakes his head. "Hurt, huh? Sounds like an awful lot of not-hurt-anymore is going on."

Fast and There

"Let me see that ankle." Dad examines it a moment, to Ella's *ows*.

It's swollen and eggplant purple. "At least it's your favorite color," I joke to Ella.

He scoops her up in his arms like a firefighter and carries her into the car. "We'd better get to the ER. I'll call your parents on the way."

As we drive to the hospital, Dad calls the exercise place and tells them to find Ella's mom. In fifteen minutes, all of us meet up in the ER waiting room, and Mrs. Fuentes is thanking my dad and me. Then the nurse calls Ella and her mom back to the emergency room, where you have to be family of the patient.

"Can't I pretend we're sisters?" I ask.

"We don't need to pretend," says Ella. "And as your sister, can I ask you a favor? Can you go to the gym and help decorate?" She hands me her phone. "All the decorations I made are on Google Drive. You can print them out again and hang them up. Well, except for the streamers."

I look at Dad. "Is this okay?"

"It's fine," Dad agrees.

"Sure, then."

"Thank you," says Ella. "I mean it."

"Feel better. I want to write on your cast, if you get one!" The doors swish close and Ella, even though she's hobbling down the hall and wincing, blows me a kiss, and mouths, "I-L-Y!"

And I mouth, "I-L-Y!" back.

Dad glances at me. "I'm proud of you, Karma. You did the right thing. You called. That was a very good decision. You used good judgment."

"See, Dad. Phones aren't evil."

"No, they aren't," he says. "They have a purpose. Many, actually. So you need to be dropped off at the gym?"

"Yes."

Did I really say that? That I was going to help decorate the gym with a bunch of girls who probably hate my guts?

Yes, I did. For Ella, I'd do anything.

"One last thing." As Dad pulls up to the school, I say, "I have some advice for you. If you're cycling and you see these cute little white, stuffed animal–looking dogs that are about twelve inches high, go in the exact opposite direction. Otherwise they could ruin your ride."

Dad grins. "I'll keep that in mind."

My Stats:
2 crazy dogs in the park who think they're vampire wolves or something
1 phone—Ella's, not mine
1 injured ankle—Ella's, not mine
6 muddified streamers
1 awesome dad
1 best friend who's the best best friend in the world

Mood: Not bad but a little nervous

25

Storming the Gym

My dirt-speckled sneakers splash in the puddles outside school. Bailey, of course, will be wearing a pair of new flats. I take a deep breath and peek into the gym. I'm in jeans and a regular T-shirt. Nothing special. I feel a little plain, a little dumb, but I try not to think about it.

Megan sweeps the floor while Janel drags tables around the perimeter. A bunch of girls who I don't know so well are flitting around setting chips and pretzels out on a big, long table. There are little tables where people can sit in groups around the edge of the gym. The DJ is setting up on the stage. Kids are pulling out the legs on long tables. Others carry other tables and line them up along the wall. More volunteers set out paper cups and a lemonade dispenser. Teacher chaperones help kids bring in bags of ice and snacks from the cars.

Meanwhile, Bailey stands in the center hunching her shoulders. She wears new white tennis shoes but the rest of her looks tired. Her eyes aren't sparkly. There are rings under them. Maybe you can't always sleep if you want to be perfect.

Bailey glances at her phone and then at Megan. "Where is Ella? She's supposed to be here with the decorations." Bailey's voice rises in panic. "I know she's late, but people, this is ridiculous!"

"She can't come." I move out of the doorway and head toward Bailey.

Both Bailey and Megan whirl around. Bailey stares at me, blinking. Janel puts down her table and eyes me suspiciously

"I'm here," I say in a louder voice. "Because Ella is in the hospital."

The expression on Bailey's face completely changes. "Oh my gosh. Is she okay?"

"I think so. But she fell off her bike and hurt her ankle." I take a deep breath. "So she asked me to help."

For a moment I expected Bailey to shout "YOU? YOU are going to help?"

But she doesn't. She doesn't say anything at all.

Until

Bailey smiles and says, "Wow, Karma. Thanks for coming. So you have Ella's decorations?"

"That's the thing. When she fell, all of the streamers and stars and moons fell into a puddle and got—"

"Muddified?" finishes Janel.

"Exactly," I say.

Bailey pulls on her chin and stares at dozens of pieces of strings dangling from the ceiling. "We've spent hours hanging those." She glances up at a clock in the gym. "The dance is starting in forty minutes. And without the moons and stars, it's going to look so dumb."

"It's all right. I've got Ella's phone."

"Okaaaaay." Bailey's eyebrows rise up into a question.

"She has all of the stars and moons on Google Drive."

"Awesome," says Bailey.

"Yeah." I pull out Ella's phone. "We can look at them now."

Bailey pops her hand over her mouth. "Her phone's all cracked."

Megan leans forward. "If it's all wet, you're supposed to put it in a bag of rice."

"Yeah, but I just used it." I press the on button.

Nothing happens.

It's time for me to beg. "C'mon. C'mon, please."

Megan clucks her tongue. "Seriously. Rice works. I thought you'd know, of all people."

I try again, even shake it. "Wake up!" More nothing. "Nooooo!"

Behind me the kids hanging lights turn to gape. Even some chaperones hauling a carton of bottled water stop to stare.

Bailey closes her eyes. "Really, Karma? Everything you touch gets messed up."

My heart sinks. "Not everything. We can still get those moons and stars printed out."

"The school computer lab," says Bailey.

"Perfect!" I twist my hair into a bun and rub the back of my sweaty neck.

Bailey clutches her clipboard. "Okay, I'll go with Karma and . . ." She looks at Megan and Janel.

"I'll check on the volunteers," says Megan.

"I'll look after the food," says Janel.

"Excellent." Bailey hands them her clipboard. "Just check things off the master list. Mrs. Grayson's in the parking lot unloading water bottles from her car." Mr. Brindle, the head custodian, examines the electrical cords for the DJ station.

"Anything else, Bail?" asks Megan as Bailey takes a few steps toward the door. I trail behind.

"Mrs. Grayson said to check the floor for screws, nails, anything sharp. Sometimes kids take off their shoes when they dance, and we don't want anyone getting hurt. Maybe you could grab a few volunteers and do a quick sweep with the push brooms before we go?"

"Sure thing," says Megan.

As I take in all of the scurrying volunteers and adults transforming our gym into a magical dance hall, I start to think that Bailey really could run something big when she gets older, like a hotel, or maybe a country.

> Sealed

We trudge over to the main hallway and pull open the door. But it doesn't open. Bailey tugs and the handle rattles, but the door's locked. A sheen of sweat shines on

Bailey's face and smeared eye shadow. And for the first time, her hair doesn't look so neat. It's kind off-center. It makes me happy to know that sometimes, maybe once a century, Bailey isn't so perfect.

"Unless we get those stars and moons up quick, we're themeless," Bailey says frantically.

"Custodian," I say, snapping my fingers. We race back to the gym and skid into the room. I flag down Mr. Brindle, who's holding an extension cord. "Can you help us?" I ask.

Bailey says, "We need to get into the computer lab. It's an emergency."

Mr. Brindle plugs in the extension cord. "Always something," he grumbles.

I look at Bailey in panic.

"No worries." Mr. Brindle smiles. "Come with me."

The Plan

The second Mr. Brindle lets us into the lab, I fly to a computer and get onto Google Drive. I stare at Ella's stars and moons. Most of them are regular-looking, but she also has the funky ones with swirling colors and big eyes wearing sunglasses and wings. These are the stars and moons she made before I told her to make the regular kind. They really are cool, though. Sometimes it's good to save things, and that makes me think about the historical society. On an impulse, I print them out along with the regular ones.

Bailey smiles at the goofy ones. "These are fun," she says, glancing at the computer screen.

"I agree."

She points to something else on Google Drive. "What's that?"

I shrug and click past it. "Nothing."

"It says photo collage. It's not nothing. I want to see."

I open it up. It's the photo collage I made. The ones showing Bailey singing, Janel dancing, Ella drawing, Milton P. doing LEGOs, and even Auggie playing ukulele.

"These are awesome," says Bailey. "I always knew you were a great photographer."

I can't help smiling.

"Print them all out," says Bailey. "It goes with our theme—*Shoot for the moon*. We can put them up."

"Really?" I look up at the clock on the wall. "The dance starts in thirty-five minutes."

"We'll make it in time."

So I print out the photos, too.

We sprint back into the gym and pass Mrs. Grayson and some volunteers hauling water. "Oh, you got the decorations," she says. "Perfect."

"Of course," says Bailey.

Mrs. Grayson heads over to the refreshments table, and Bailey hands out stars and moons to volunteers to hang on the strings. Soon we are admiring how great everything looks. The lights dim. The disco ball is up and spinning. Dots of light swim around the gym. A steady beat pounds out of the speakers. The dance starts in thirty minutes. And everything does look awesome.

Suddenly I see someone I'm not expecting to see. It's Ella, on crutches, hobbling into the gym. She wears a supercute crop top over skinny jeans, but she looks pale. I rush over.

"Are you okay?" I ask.

She nods and I run to get her a chair to settle down in. Bailey pushes a table in front of us and sets down a cup of water. Immediately Janel and Megan rush over.

"Oh my gosh," says Bailey. "Is your leg broken?"

Ella shakes her head. "My ankle's just sprained." I think about giving back her broken phone, but I want to wait for the right moment. If there is such a thing.

"Does it hurt?" asks Janel.

"Just a little." Ella brushes her long dark hair off her shoulders. "No dancing. Just watching."

"I'm superglad it's not broken," says Megan.

Megan glances at the stars and moons as volunteers continue to tape them onto the strings. "Hey, you printed out all of them."

"Yes," I say.

"They *all* look so good, especially the stars with sunglasses."

Ella smiles, and that's when I start to push the messed-up phone out of my pocket, but Ella stares at something else. The stack of papers in my left hand. "What are those?" she asks.

"Just some photos I took," I mumble.

She bends over to peer at them. "Portraits, Karma. These are really good."

I push her phone back into my pocket as Ella shuffles through the photos. "This one of Janel is awesome," she says. "Her jeans are sparkling with light. How did you do that?"

"I'm not so sure." Other girls are coming over and poring over the photos, *ooh*ing and *ahh*ing. And suddenly I'm thinking about the portraits I'm going to do of the founders of the synagogue. That's going to be so cool.

In the gym, Bailey smiles at my portraits. "They're amazing. Put them up, people. Tape them up to the walls."

"On any bare strings," adds Megan.

Bailey surveys the room. "Much better than crepe paper and store-bought decorations. I-L-Y!"

"I-L-Y!" says Megan.

"I-L-Y," says Janel.

"I-L-Y," says Ella, which is best of all.

Not Really Shattered

The gym looks truly transformed. My photos decorate the paper-lined walls. Ella's moons and stars spin around on strings. Tiny, sparkly blue-and-white lights weave around the tables and along walls. The DJ plays upbeat, danceable tunes. It's 6:15. The dance starts in fifteen minutes. The volunteers have mostly stopped working since everything is about done. Mrs. Grayson collects a few boxes from the pizzas that were eaten earlier and unstacks folding chairs. A few other kids flit around, excitedly chatting, taking a break before the dance officially starts.

Ella sits at a table so she can rest her leg. "I'm so glad you're all right," I say, munching on some chips. "And that your bone isn't broken." Then I stare at the floor. "But your phone—" I pull it out of my pocket. "It's not so great." I meet Ella's eyes. "It's not even turning on now."

Ella leans forward to examine it. She cups the phone in her hands, staring at the web of cracks. The corners of her mouth pull down into a frown. Bailey and the Bees sit on the other side of the gym by the ticket table, counting change. I hold my breath.

"I'm so sorry about what happened," I finally say. "I'm sorry about everything."

"It'll be fine. Anyway, my parents have insurance for the phone." She smiles as if it's all really okay.

"So we'll both be phoneless for a while, since Flippie doesn't count."

"Actually, you won't be phoneless." Ella grabs her plaid tote bag and opens it. "Because you, Karma Cooper, have"—she hands me a phone—"this."

"What?!!!!!!!" I gasp at my raspberry-colored cell. "Floyd! But how? I don't understand."

"Life is full of miracles." Ella laughs as she watches me brush my fingers over the screen.

"Oh my gosh. I love you! I-L-Y! I-L-Y!"

Across the gym, girls turn to look at us.

I blink a few times and rub my eyes to see if I'm imagining this. But no, Floyd sits in my own hot little hands. Yes, truly hot because the gym swells with heat and stuffiness. But it's okay. All the decorations and kids and music fade into the background.

"Seriously. How did you get my phone?"

Ella smiles a huge smile. "Your mom came by the hospital to see me. When she found out I was going to the dance, she wanted me to give it you. She told me that she's really proud of you, Karma."

I search her eyes. "Are you serious? My mom said that?"

She leans forward. "Uh-huh. She knew that your flip phone was limited. She said you can have Floyd back for good, with certain conditions."

"Wow. I just. Can't. Believe. This." Laughing, I jump and start dancing around in a circle. I close my eyes and press the phone to my cheek again. A group of volunteers begins gathering around. They stand near us, whooping and clapping. "I've been waiting for you forever." I give Floyd a kiss.

Ella snorts. "Are you going to slow dance with Floyd?"

"Maybe."

She gives me a sly look. "Or you could slow dance with Auggie."

I make a face. But for some crazy reason my heart thumps faster as I think about his sky-blue eyes.

"Ewww. Auggie and Karma." Ella claps her hands and Bailey and the Bees rush over from the ticket table. They slip past the girls gathered around me as I continue to slow dance with Floyd. Ella looks on, laughing.

"What's happening?" asks Bailey.

"She's reunited with Floyd!" shouts Megan.

"Woot!" yells Janel.

"Karma got her phone back! All right!" shouts Bailey. She throws her arms around me. And then so do Janel and Megan and Ella, until we are jumble of arms. Even the other volunteers who I don't know as well are joining our group hug.

After we break apart, Bailey whirls around, surveying the gym. "This place looks awesome. Thanks, everyone."

"Yeah," says Megan. "You guys are the best."

"Those moons and stars with sunglasses are too cute," says Janel.

"I think they should all go into the yearbook," adds Megan.

"Love, *love* the decorations." Bailey squints up at the wall at my photos of kids at our school. "I could imagine some of those in my mom's gallery. Good, Karma. Very good."

Ella and I look at each other and grin. And then I realize something. I haven't even bothered to turn on my phone.

Megan and Janel head to the gym entrance. "We're going to open the doors soon," says Megan. "It's almost time." She peers up at the clock on the wall. It's 6:20. At 6:30 everyone will swarm the gym.

Bailey grabs a bowl of chips and offers some to us. We all munch away. "Sorry that I was acting like a jerk," she says. "I just wanted it all to go perfectly."

"No, I'm sorry I was acting like a jerk," I say, biting into a chip.

Ella taps her chest. "No, sorry *I* was acting like a jerk."

"You weren't acting like a jerk," I say. "I got your phone locked up at the office, and got you in trouble."

"Yeah. True." Ella stretches out her other leg. "But I shouldn't have said some things."

"Ditto."

"Ditto on your ditto."

Bailey crunches on a chip. "Ditto on your ditto on your ditto." Then we all crack up laughing.

> ## The Crutch

It's 6:23. The dance starts in seven minutes. I take out my brush and smooth my hair. Ella sits next to me, her crutches leaning on one side of her chair. Nearby, volunteers munch on some cookies. We sit by the punch bowl.

"You look nice," says Ella.

"Thanks."

"You'll never believe what happened between me and my mother."

"What? What won't I believe?" And then suddenly I know. "Your mother caught you with make-up and stuff."

She nods.

"Oh my gosh. Did she go crazy on you?"

Ella smiles. "Karma, you can always read my mind. . . . Yes, she started screaming!"

I feel an invisible thread pull me closer to Ella—closer than we have been in a few weeks.

"It happened on Monday, actually. When I called my mom to get my phone from the office, I forgot that I had on make-up. Mascara, some blush. A little eye shadow. And um, my change of clothes." Ella shakes her head. "She was so mad. She said she couldn't trust me anymore. And then she started crying. It was terrible."

"So that's why this week you weren't changing into your skinny jeans or wearing make-up."

"Yeah, she took it all away." A smile grows on Ella's face. "But I got it back."

"What happened?"

"Mom apologized in the ER. She doesn't want me to keep secrets. She said I can wear a little mascara to school as long as I don't glob it on. And on special occasions I can wear eye shadow."

"And tonight is a special occasion."

"Exactly." Ella bats her eyelashes.

"Are you sure it was your mother?"

Ella nods as she leans forward.

"Maybe you should fall off a bike and almost break your ankle more often."

"Maybe . . . and maybe not. It really hurt."

Anytime

Four minutes before the dance starts, the music booms. A few kids wander in, and the volunteers cluster around the table to munch on snacks. A couple of teacher chaperones chat together in the corner.

As Mrs. Grayson props open a side door, a breeze flows into the gym. "It still feels stuffy," she says, "but it will cool down soon."

I stand next to Ella. "You can borrow my phone anytime."

"Thanks," she says. "You're the best."

I smile and motion toward myself. "Tell me more about how I'm the best."

"The bestest best friend."

My smile grows bigger, even though beads of sweat drip down my neck. I finally have my best friend back.

Bailey yells at some kids from across the gym, "You guys, can you please get over to the ticket booth? We're going to need more people. The doors are about to open."

"It's almost showtime," I say.

"Yup," says Ella.

I peer outside the open side door to the picnic benches. The rain stopped.

"Do you want to sit down on one of the picnic benches outside for a bit before the dance starts?"

"Sure," says Ella.

We walk around the basketball hoop toward the side

exit—or rather, I walk and Ella hobbles. Leaning in, I whisper to Ella, "You know, I didn't die without my phone, and not having Snappypic. It was kind of easy— once I got used to it."

"I know." She smiles and I smile back as I tuck my phone safely away in my back pocket. The sun sets in the dusky sky.

And together, we walk out of the stuffy gym and into the cool air. Gazing up, I see a honey-yellow moon peeking through the clouds.

My Stats:
0 followers
0 people I'm following
0 LIKES of nothing
1 real phone back, with limits
1 camera, and 1 cool family
1 very cool BFF and lots of new friends

Mood: Not bad, not bad at all—Awesome!

ACKNOWLEDGMENTS

An epic number of LIKES to:

My warm and wise editor, Alyson Heller, who "liked" Karma from birth and nudged her to put down her phone and become an archivist.

The other members of the Aladdin team (from managing ed to marketing and publicity to the art and design folks). Again, Karma (and I) thank you.

Victoria Wells Arms, agent extraordinaire. Maybe it's the fact that we both have three kids (and a love for *Harriet the Spy*) that makes you my tween spirit guide.

Rachel Rodriguez, critique partner, word ninja, and, like me, endless blabbermouth.

My Napa writing group, the wine and dessert divas: Jenny Pessereau, Sherry Smith, and Leslie Farwell. Eternal gratitude doesn't even come close.

Lisa Gottfried and her students at New Tech High School. Your LIKE videos are attention-getting enough to even grace Karma's Snappypic page. ☺

Roberta and Gerry Schlesinger, who each and every summer feed and clothe and house and entertain and educate their grandson (my youngest son) and provide a treasured writing holiday for me. Thank you, thank you!

Alexandria Lafaye, for being my friend, my teacher and my supporter since graduate school, which seems now like a galaxy far, far away.

The Hollins Faculty critique group, who had a look at the first chapter of *Queen of Likes* and requested more, more, more!

Erin Dealey, who gave me early input when Karma's name was still Nolie.

Steven Arvanites, who never said no, even when I asked for the moon. Okay, I didn't really ask for the moon, but you would get it for me if I did.

Becca Leifer, Carol and Natalie Guthrie. Because at some point all of you mentored me in all things tween and phone and social and media.

My niece Stella Eisenberg. I appreciate your early read and Grandmom Reta's youthful spirit and writerly instincts!

Deb Wallace and Cindy Kirkland. I hope Karma learns to treat her BFFs as well as you treat each other and everyone you touch.

A big shout out to Rabbi Lee Bycel. If Karma were attending Congregation Beth Shalom, she wouldn't have skipped the service to hang out in the bathroom on her phone. She'd be live blogging the service no doubt.

Nancy Levenberg, Executive Director of the Napa County Historical Society, for so graciously allowing me to observe the marvelous goings-on in her world. And Alexandra Brown, Research Librarian, and the team of volunteers, for tutoring me in all things archival.

Ari Eisenberg, teen crooner (and son of mine), for writing the song "Queen of Likes." Check it out on SoundCloud! And speaking of sons, all of my sons—Jonah, Ari, and Micah, have endured me reading them endless variations of the opening and various chapters of the book. Thank you for being such good sports.

Matt Eisenberg, husband and official Costco shopper for our family of boys with supersize appetites, I have a supersize amount of love for you, not to mention for large bags of chips and turkey jerky.

Check out these great titles from Aladdin M!X:

ALADDINMIX.COM

EBOOK EDITIONS ALSO AVAILABLE

 | From Aladdin | KIDS.SimonandSchuster.com